WARRIOR'S WRATH

A Dark Ages Scottish Romance

**The Pict Wars
Book Three**

JAYNE CASTEL

Historical Romances by Jayne Castel

DARK AGES BRITAIN

The Kingdom of the East Angles series
Dark Under the Cover of Night (Book One)
Nightfall till Daybreak (Book Two)
The Deepening Night (Book Three)
*The Kingdom of the East Angles: The Complete
Series*

The Kingdom of Mercia series
The Breaking Dawn (Book One)
Darkest before Dawn (Book Two)
Dawn of Wolves (Book Three)
The Kingdom of Mercia: The Complete Series

The Kingdom of Northumbria series
The Whispering Wind (Book One)
Wind Song (Book Two)
Lord of the North Wind (Book Three)
The Kingdom of Northumbria: The Complete Series

DARK AGES SCOTLAND

The Warrior Brothers of Skye series
Blood Feud (Book One)
Barbarian Slave (Book Two)
Battle Eagle (Book Three)
The Warrior Brothers of Skye: The Complete Series

The Pict Wars series
Warrior's Heart (Book One)
Warrior's Secret (Book Two)
Warrior's Wrath (Book Three)
The Pict Wars: The Complete Series

Novellas
Winter's Promise

MEDIEVAL SCOTLAND

The Brides of Skye series
The Beast's Bride (Book One)
The Outlaw's Bride (Book Two)
The Rogue's Bride (Book Three)
The Brides of Skye: The Complete Series

The Sisters of Kilbride series
Unforgotten (Book One)
Awoken (Book Two)
Fallen (Book Three)
Claimed (Epilogue novella)

The Immortal Highland Centurions series
Maximus (Book One)
Cassian (Book Two)
Draco (Book Three)
The Laird's Return (Epilogue festive novella)

Epic Fantasy Romances by Jayne Castel

Light and Darkness series
Ruled by Shadows (Book One)
The Lost Swallow (Book Two)
Path of the Dark (Book Three)
Light and Darkness: The Complete Series

A warrior driven by wrath. A woman willing to sacrifice herself for peace. A destiny neither can escape. Revenge and fated love in Ancient Scotland.

Talor mac Donnel wants revenge. Consumed by hate, he goes into occupied territory seeking vengeance for his slain sister. But Talor's plan goes awry when, instead of killing the man responsible for his sister's death, he is taken captive.

Mor is tired of war. Her people have swept across The Winged Isle, leaving carnage behind them. Mor is a warrior, yet all she wants now is to lay down her weapons and live in peace. And when a crazed enemy warrior breaks into their broch and tries to slay her father, she makes a decision that will change everything between their people.

The instant Talor locks gazes with his enemy's proud daughter, Mor, everything he thought he believed about life and love starts to unravel. Together, they have the chance to bring peace to their war-torn isle—but only if he is able to let go of the past.

***

To my husband, Tim. With all my love.

***

Maps of Scotland and The Winged Isle

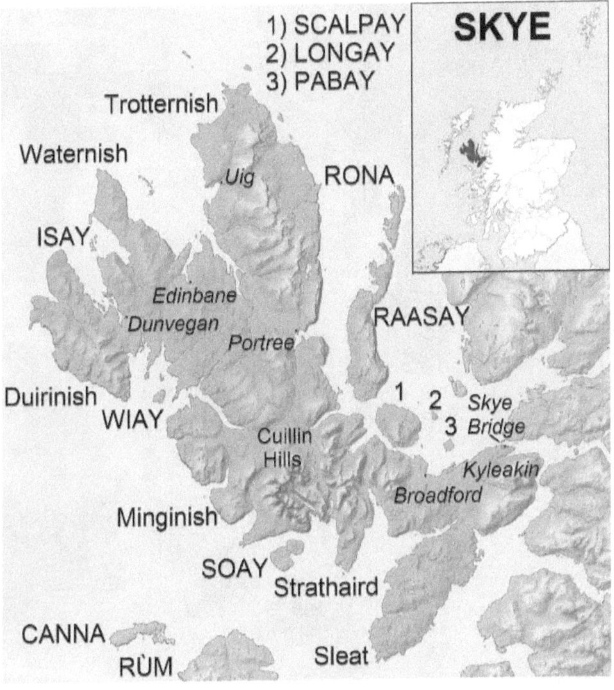

THE
WINGED
ISLE
(4TH CENTURY AD)
DUN
SKUDIBURGH
DUN
GRIANAN
THE
STAG
DUN
VEGAN
THE WOLF
DUN
ARDTRECK
THE
BLACK CUILLINS
LOCHANS OF
THE FAIR FOLK
MAINLAND
THE EAGLE
THE
RED HILL
DUN RINGILL
KYLEAKIN
THE BOAR
AN TEANGA

Your feet will bring you to where your heart is.
~ Irish Proverb.

Prologue

Sleep Well My Brothers

Mid-Winter Fire—389 AD

*Dun Ringill—Territory of The Serpent
The Winged Isle (The Isle of Skye)*

SHE LEFT THE fort alone, without telling anyone of her destination.

An icy wind blew in from the north, bringing a sprinkle of snowflakes with it—the first of the winter. Noting the turn in the weather, Mor momentarily questioned her decision to ride out this afternoon. Reining up her shaggy grey pony, she cast a glance over her shoulder at the squat bulk of Dun Ringill behind her, dark against the choppy waters of Loch Slapin. The sky to the south was still clear, although it would not likely stay that way.

This won't take long, she reassured herself. *I'll be home by nightfall.*

Mor's mouth thinned as her gaze lingered upon the broch and the high stone walls protecting it. *Home.* Would she ever feel that way about this place? She had to admit The Winged Isle possessed a wild beauty. Her father professed to love it, yet Dun Ringill had come at a high price.

Mor's chest constricted. *There are so few of us left now.*

Turning away from Dun Ringill, she urged the pony on, squeezing her calves against its flanks, and the beast broke into a choppy canter. The wind caught at the fur-lined hood protecting Mor's head, tearing it back. Her thick auburn hair flew free, and the wind stung her cheeks, yet Mor paid it no mind.

She had delayed this trip, but would not wait any longer. Mid-Winter Fire was upon them now, and the Long Night was the right time to lay her brothers to rest. There had been no burial for either Dunchadh or Tamhas mac Cathal, for their bodies had never been recovered. As such, Mor had not had the chance to bid either of them farewell properly, to see them safely to the Otherworld. But this afternoon she would.

Mor rode north-east, cutting across a sea of undulating grassy hills toward the outlines of great peaks that thrust into the darkening sky. An oak wood lay under the shadow of the nearest mountain, nestled in a valley between two steep hills. Her people's bandruí—seer—Old Murdina had told Mor of the forest, for she had traveled there to collect herbs. Oak woods were sacred places; there had been one near the village where her people once dwelt upon the mainland. As children, Mor and her brothers had played there.

Slowing her pony to a walk, Mor entered the woods. The snow was starting to fall in earnest now, and the weather had closed in, obscuring the bulk of the mountain looming above her.

She rode amongst the trees. The oaks had lost the last of their autumn cloaks, the leaves forming a rotting carpet beneath her pony's feet. Even so, the trees provided a barrier from the wind and snow, and Mor breathed in the tranquility.

How she missed the forests of the mainland. Most of The Winged Isle was bleak and barren with vast moorlands and jagged mountains. However, there were pockets, like this one, of oak, hazel, birch, and pine hidden in valleys throughout—you just had to know where to look.

Mor traveled deep into the valley, to where the oaks were the oldest, finally drawing her pony up before the biggest of them: a huge spreading tree that sat near the banks of a trickling burn.

A smile tugged at Mor's mouth at the sight of the great oak, penetrating the mantle of sadness that had cloaked her of late. Her people called this a 'mother oak'—one that had lived many lifetimes of men and would stand to see many more. It lightened her heart to set eyes on such a tree again.

"Old Murdina was right," she murmured as her gaze rested upon it. "You *are* magnificent."

The seer had told her that such a tree dwelt in the heart of this valley. A 'mother oak' was a place where bandruís consulted with the Gods and waited for divine inspiration.

It was the perfect place to lay her brothers' spirits to rest.

Tearing her attention from the tree, Mor opened the satchel that she wore slung across her front and reached inside. She withdrew two objects—the only things that remained of Dunchadh and Tamhas.

The first was a small bone-handled knife. Dunchadh had made it for Mor years earlier and had carved a serpent into the handle. It was one of her favorite knives. Although too small for throwing, she used it for eating or preparing food. The second object was a squat figurine of The Mother. She was the Goddess of enlightenment and feminine energy—the bringer of change. Tamhas had kept the figurine in his alcove and prayed to it every evening.

Staring down at the two objects, Mor's vision blurred. This was all she had of her brothers. What had happened to them after they had fallen? No doubt the enemy had burned their corpses; they would not have been buried in cairns like their forefathers had, and the thought made her throat ache.

Dunchadh was three winters Mor's elder. Strong, bold, and charismatic, he had dominated any space he entered. Tamhas was the youngest of the three of them. He'd had a quieter, more intense character than Dunchadh and had forever dwelt in his brother's shadow.

Both of them had fallen at Balintur, a fortified village half a day's journey north of Dun Ringill—although not during the same battles. Dunchadh had been slain when the army of the united tribes had attacked in late summer, taking back the village, and Tamhas had died barely a month earlier when their people had laid siege to Balintur.

Mor approached the tree and knelt before it. Reaching out, she placed a palm upon the rough bark of the wide trunk and closed her eyes.

An ache rose under her breast bone, crushing in its intensity.

Gods how she missed her brothers.

She longed to hear Dunchadh's booming laugh, or to watch Tamhas favor her with one of his enigmatic smiles. They had left the mainland together and fought side-by-side through a number of campaigns.

But now, they had left her alone, and Mor felt like a tree stripped of all its leaves without them.

Opening her eyes, Mor laid the knife and the figurine at the roots of the oak.

I should have brought Da with me, she thought suddenly, guilt filtering through her. With a sigh, Mor sat back on her heels. Aye, she could have, although a dark cloud dogged Cathal mac Calum's steps these days. He suffered from a constant ill-temper ever since Tamhas's death.

He gnashed his teeth and raged about revenge, swore that he would make every last warrior of the united tribes suffer for robbing him of his sons. And he had expected Mor to share his rage—yet she did not.

A hollowness had settled within her after the disaster at Balintur. They had returned to Dun Ringill, defeated, their numbers decimated, and she had begun to wonder what the point to all of this was.

Even if they turned things around now, Dunchadh and Tamhas were not here to share their victory.

War. It suddenly seemed pointless. Mor was a warrior. Like her mother before her, she had been raised to wield a pike and a sword. She knew how to throw knives, how to bring down a warrior with a bow and arrow. Those skills had served her well over the years, had kept her alive. But now, as she lowered her gaze to the knife and figurine, she wondered at the value of those abilities.

"I know you died warriors' deaths," she whispered to her brothers. "But I miss you all the same." Tears trickled down her cheeks, yet Mor did not brush them away. "Da is set on avenging you, but that doesn't feel right to me." The words seemed traitorous, although there was no one here to listen but the 'mother oak'. "I wish we could live in peace with the people of this isle." Mor's voice caught as she said these words. "Is that wrong?"

Only the whine of the wind answered her. Mor craned her neck up, looking through the bare branches above at the sky. She had barely noticed that the snow fell heavily now, penetrating the canopy of oaks and settling upon the shoulders of her fur cloak. It was time to return to Dun Ringill.

Blinking away the tears that continued to flow, Mor rose to her feet. She did not want to leave this oak thicket; if the weather had been mild, she would have lingered a while. But night fell early this time of year, and she did not want her father to worry.

Drawing in a deep, steadying breath, Mor reached out and placed her hand once more on the oak trunk. She could feel the tree's age and strength vibrating against her palm. "Sleep well my brothers," she murmured.

Chapter One

It Must Be Done

Winter—390 AD
Territory of The Eagle

One month later ...

IT WAS A journey he would never return from.

Each footstep took him farther from his family, farther from his friends. The knowledge that he would never see any of them again felt like a boulder in his gut, but Talor did not look back, did not take his eyes from the southern horizon.

Snow fluttered down from the darkening sky. It had already formed a thick white crust over the ground. His pony sank up to its feathery fetlocks in the drifts. Soon night would fall, obscuring the land even further. Yet Talor carried a torch aloft, and he knew this land as well as the lines on his father's face. He could find his way to Dun Ringill blind-folded and drunk.

Still, only a lackwit would set out on a journey on an eve like this.

A lackwit—or a man consumed by revenge.

Talor mac Donnel had thought of nothing else over the past two moons. Thoughts of his fallen sister had plagued every waking moment, as had fantasies of what he would do to the man who had slain her: Cathal mac Calum, the chieftain of The Serpent tribe.

Cathal's warriors had attacked the village of Balintur, had nearly brought Talor's people to their knees. Fortunately, help had arrived before that had happened. But it hadn't been soon enough for Bonnie.

The memory of his half-sister, fighting valiantly amongst the mob of men and women twice her size, rose unbidden. She had been small but fierce, the quickest of them all. But the moment he had seen a huge auburn-haired man stride toward her, sword swinging, Talor had known brave Bonnie was doomed.

Cathal had enjoyed it too. Till his dying day, Talor would never forget the grimace of wild joy on the warrior's face as he cut Bonnie down.

Blinking hard to dislodge the snowflakes settling on his eyelashes, Talor gave his head a shake and focused on his surroundings once more. He needed to keep his wits about him. Despite the snow, The Serpent would have scouts out as he neared Dun Ringill. To avoid them, he had taken a longer, more difficult route, along the coast rather than the more common path over softly undulating hills.

The snow swirled in, thicker now, and Talor breathed a soft curse. In many ways the snow was his ally, for it hid him from view, yet at the same time he didn't want to accidentally ride off the clifftop. His pony, a heavyset, dappled grey stallion he had named Luath—Ash—blended in with the surroundings this evening. The pony plodded forward doggedly, head lowered, although its furry ears flicked around. Like Talor, the pony was taking in its surroundings, senses attuned to anything amiss.

Shifting the torch to his left hand, Talor shook out a cramping muscle in his right bicep. There would be a full moon out tonight once the black curtain of night drew over the world, but with the snow he would not be able to take advantage of it. Hence, why he had brought a torch.

Around him the gloaming settled, draining the last of the light from the sky. The snow continued to flutter and swirl, and Luath plowed on. They were not far from where rocky cliffs plunged down to stony beaches and a churning grey sea. However, due to the weather, Talor did not want to ride too close to the edge of them. He'd had to slow his pony, as there were moments when he could not see more than a yard or two ahead.

A wind gusted in from the north, biting through Talor's layers of clothing to the warm flesh beneath. He had deliberately dressed for the weather in thick leather breeches, three layers of tunics—one of which was woolen—a leather vest, and heavy fur-lined boots. Nonetheless, the chill drove through the fabric.

Talor's breath steamed before him, and he was glad of the pony's warmth against his legs. Just his luck that tonight looked to be one of the coldest yet of the bitter season. Fortunately, Luath was built for such weather; the hardy pony barely seemed to notice the chill.

The evening drew on, and a smothering darkness settled. Talor's world shrank to the guttering glow of his pitch torch, which illuminated the steadily falling snow. Eventually though, Talor reached his destination, guiding Luath down a slope to a pebbly beach.

Swinging down from the pony's back, Talor stroked Luath's neck, his fingers sliding into the stallion's plush winter coat. "This is where we part ways, lad," he murmured.

Luath snorted and nudged Talor, looking for the treats he knew the warrior often carried on him.

"No carrots, tonight," Talor replied, his mouth curving into a grim smile. "You're always thinking of your belly, aren't you?" He stroked the pony's ears, his throat constricting.

The reality of what he was doing fully hit him then.

He was leaving everything behind. Never again would he gallop Luath over the bare hills of his homeland, the wind stinging his cheeks. Never again would he race his cousin Muin in the summer games, or spar with him in the training ring. He would never hear his father's low voice or hear his step-mother, Eithni, play the harp again. He would not see his surviving half-sister, Eara, grow up.

The grip on Talor's throat tightened.

Aye, he was turning his back on it all, leaving behind everything he loved. But ever since Bonnie's death, his world had been shrouded in grey. He had felt like a ghost, residing amongst the living, but not interacting with them.

Muin and his love, Ailene, had wed just a few days earlier, but although he had been happy for them, he had been barely able to raise a smile. Ailene was also Talor's cousin, although she was not related to Muin; rather, her and Talor's mothers had been sisters. Tragically, both women had died young. Talor's mother had died of 'the birthing sickness' just after giving birth to Talor, while Ailene had lost her mother in childhood to a wasting illness.

Muin and Ailene's handfasting had been a joyous affair. The whole population of Balintur—where his people had taken refuge over the past months—had celebrated the event with feasting, drinking, and dancing.

But Talor had stood apart from it all.

He had known that evening, as he watched Muin and Ailene dance around the fire, that something inside him was broken. The only thing that would fix it was avenging his sister's death—killing the man who had slain her.

Thoughts of Cathal mac Calum's grinning face snapped Talor out of his reverie, chasing away the grief that thoughts of leaving his kin had brought forth.

Removing Luath's saddle and bridle, Talor slapped the pony on the rump. He carried no pack, no provisions.

He needed none for this journey. Instead, he had brought an arsenal of weapons with him. He wore a quiver and longbow over his back, a sword at his waist, and he had a number of blades strapped to his body. "Time to return to Balintur, lad," he said, watching the pony toss his head. Luath liked to be free, although the beast hesitated, its dark eyes fixing upon Talor.

A lump rose in Talor's throat. "Go now," he said. "We'll meet again."

Aye, most likely in the afterlife.

Still, the pony did not move. Instead, it gave a soft whicker, almost as if it sensed his bleak mood.

"Go!" Talor slapped the stallion on the rump once more, harder this time.

With a squeal, Luath jumped back, turned, and plowed up the slope, disappearing into the swirling snow.

Talor watched him go, his throat thickening once more. Luath was a canny pony—he would find his way back to Balintur.

Enough of this, he chastised himself. *It must be done.*

His pitch torch had almost burned out now so he cast it aside. He would brave the rest of the journey without it; he knew the path to the fort from this stretch of shore well. He would not need a torch to light his way.

Moving blindly along the pebbly beach, finding his way by tracing his fingers along the edges of the boulders that studded the landward side, Talor moved steadily south. It had been difficult at first, without his torch, to see anything at all, but his eyes quickly adjusted to the darkness. He could see the emptiness to his right—where the sea lay—and sensed the bulk of the rising headland to his left.

And soon after, he spied a glow of light to the south-east.

Another grim smile stretched Talor's mouth. Dun Ringill lay just a short distance ahead.

Now that he traveled on foot, the cold had dug its claws deep. His toes inside his fur-lined boots were starting to tingle, and Talor buried his fingers under his armpits to keep them warm; he would need feeling in his hands for the next stage in his plan.

Eventually, the glow up ahead became more defined: a row of fires burning atop the walls lining the fort. Climbing up, his hands and feet sliding over icy rocks, Talor craned his neck. He could just make out the shadow of the broch beyond the walls; its solid, squat shape rising up into the darkness.

Home.

Talor's right hand clenched, moving instinctively to the knife he wore strapped to his right thigh. Those Serpents had taken his home; they had swept in like a plague of locusts, had forced his people out of their fort and claimed it as their own.

Not for much longer.

The day after Muin and Ailene's handfasting, the four chieftains representing the tribes that inhabited The Winged Isle had met. Varar of The Boar had even traveled up from An Teanga to attend the meeting. They had decided that they would launch an attack on Dun Ringill later in the month, once the bitterest of the winter weather had abated.

Talor had welcomed the news, although he had been torn. He wanted them to attack now, but he also needed to be the one to take Cathal mac Calum down. He did not want anyone else to end his life.

He longed to hold that shit-weasel's eye as he twisted the blade.

That was why he had done this, had left Balintur without a word to anyone. They would have tried to stop him, but he would not be stopped.

He would taste vengeance. For Bonnie.

Heart hammering, Talor shifted his gaze from the broch's dark shadow to the high stacked stone walls that surrounded the fort itself. They would be watched on all sides—all except the seaward wall.

The fort perched on the edge of a cliff, facing west out to sea. On a fine day it commanded a clear view in all directions. The seaward wall was the fort's only weakness, although only a reckless or highly skilled climber would attempt to enter Dun Ringill that way.

Talor grinned. He was both.

As bairns, he had incited his younger cousin, Muin, into many exploits. One of them had been to climb the seaward wall. It was perilous. One slip, one false move, and you risked tumbling down the cliff and dashing your brains out on the jagged rocks below.

Still, the two lads had managed the climb a few times—until their fathers discovered their antics. They had both received a sound beating afterward, and had not attempted the climb again.

Talor's gaze settled upon the high wall he intended to scale, and he began to edge his way toward the base of it. He moved slowly, deliberately, for the rocks around the base had iced over. This was going to be even more dangerous than he had thought.

Reaching the wall, Talor peered up. No fire burned directly above him; this was the right spot to climb, for the warriors who were taking the night watch would not be likely to spy an intruder slowly making his way up the wall. Stacked stone was reasonably easy to climb, even with cold-numbed fingers, for there were plenty of finger and toe holds. Nonetheless, the wall was high and would be difficult to scale.

Jaw set in determination, Talor began to climb.

He took things slowly, inching up the wall with painstaking care. As a child, he had climbed the wall barefoot, but that was not possible tonight. Moving gradually upward, Talor caught the faint snatches of conversation from warriors atop the wall; there were at least two of them on this side—closer to him than he had first thought. He would have to move fast once he reached the top.

Breathing slowly, despite the sweat that now poured off him, Talor continued to climb. His fingers and toes where completely numb, his hands and feet aching, and the muscles in his legs, upper arms, and shoulders burned. Yet he did not falter.

Eventually, Talor scaled the final feet, his fingers grasping around the top edge of the wall. Heaving in a deep breath, he hauled himself up and over, onto the narrow walkway that led around the edge.

After such a climb, all he wanted to do was collapse and suck in deep breaths of air, while thanking the Gods for watching over him.

However, there was no time for that—he would have only moments before the guards just a few yards away spotted him.

Talor dropped into a crouch, unslinging his bow from his back and notching an arrow.

An instant later a shout split the night air. One of the guards had seen him. A huge figure wrapped in fur barreled along the wall toward Talor. The scrape of iron followed as the warrior unsheathed his sword.

Talor had only moments until the man would be too close.

Hissing a curse, Talor drew back his bowstring before loosing an arrow directly at the Cruthini warrior's exposed neck.

Chapter Two

Mor's Slight

HE HAD BEEN watching her all evening, and it was starting to grate on Mor's nerves. The way she was feeling these days, she had little patience for unwanted admirers.

She knew Tormud wanted her; he had made no secret of it over the past moons. Yet he had grown bold in his attentions of late. Too bold.

Picking up her cup of ale, Mor took a measured sip. She could feel the heat of the warrior's stare as she did so, the predatory way he tracked her every movement.

Heat stirred in Mor's belly—yet it was not the heat of lust, but of anger.

Enough.

Mor shifted her gaze down the table to where the heavy-set warrior lounged, cup of ale in hand. Tormud was at least two decades her elder, yet he was fit and strong, and carried himself with the unconscious arrogance of a man who knew he was still in his prime.

His dark hair, cut brutishly short, was peppered with grey, as was the stubble that covered his bullish jaw.

Tormud's dark blue gaze was hooded this evening, his expression intense. Despite the chill weather—even the great hearth that burned in the center of the feasting hall could not keep it wholly at bay—the warrior wore a sleeveless leather vest that showed off his muscular arms. Upon his right bicep, he bore a faded blue inked mark of The Boar.

Tormud mac Alec was not one of the Cruthini. Her people were tall and loose-limbed with ruddy or brown hair, whereas Tormud—like many men of this isle—was shorter and dark-haired.

"What is it?" Mor growled out the question. She could not stand his staring any longer. Cooped up inside this broch, surrounded by restless and embittered men and women, Mor's tolerance was on a short leash this evening.

Tormud had taken to staring at her whenever their paths crossed of late, which was often as they both resided inside the broch. A confrontation between them was long overdue.

The warrior's mouth curved into a rare smile. "Isn't a man allowed to look at a comely lass?"

"Looking is one thing," Mor replied. "But staring as if you have just received a new pair of eyes and are trying them out for the first time, is another."

Tormud snorted a laugh, before he reached for a jug in the center of the table and refilled his cup. "It is not my fault if your beauty entrances me."

Mor went still. She had not expected such frankness. For a few brief moments, she did not know how to respond.

They sat alone at one of the long tables that lined the feasting hall, close to where glowing lumps of peat burned in the great hearth. A few men and women occupied the hall, although many had already retired to their alcoves for the night. Of late, the mood inside the broch was somber in the evenings, a reminder that things were looking grim indeed for their people.

Up on the platform behind them, her father and uncle sat together at the chieftain's table. Her father, Cathal, reclined upon a magnificent oaken chair. The back and armrests had been carved into the likeness of eagles, one of the many reminders that this fort had once belonged to another tribe: The Eagle.

Cathal was glowering tonight, as he often did these days, while her uncle, Artair, was shaking his head at something his brother had just said. Artair's once handsome face looked haggard this evening, deep grooves etched into it from the pain that plagued him. He had taken serious wounds to his abdomen and hip during the siege of Balintur, and two moons on was still recovering. His healing had been a slow, tortuous path, and Mor sometimes wondered if her uncle would ever return to his former self.

Turning her attention from the chieftain's table, reassured that no one had overheard Tormud's bold words, Mor frowned at The Boar warrior.

"This has to stop," she said, her voice low and firm. "Isn't it clear that I'm not interested?"

Tormud shrugged, not remotely chagrined. "No. You're proud and independent, just how I like my women."

His women.

Tormud had joined her tribe over twenty years earlier, around the time of Mor's birth. He had taken part in the attack on the Great Wall to the south, which had broken the Caesars' last seat of power in the lands of the Cruthini. After that he had wed one of her tribe—her aunt. Mor's aunt Nessa had been a warrior, a fierce woman who had fought in many battles, but who had died in childbirth, taking the bairn with her.

Tormud had never re-wed, although Mor knew that he had taken plenty of lovers over the years.

"I repeat, I'm not interested," Mor said coldly, her fingers tightening around her cup. She thought then of her brother Tamhas. He had never liked Tormud. Unlike Dunchadh, who had been of a more trusting disposition, Tamhas had possessed a watchful, suspicious temperament. Perhaps because of this, he had noted that Tormud was also a man who observed much and said little. Mor shared Tamhas's view of The Boar.

Where did Tormud's allegiances truly lie? Her father trusted the warrior blindly, but she had always wondered if he was right to do so.

Still watching her with a predatory intensity that was starting to make Mor's skin crawl, Tormud leaned forward. "Why? Do you think I'm too old for you?"

Mor took another sip from her cup. "Aye, among other things."

"And what are they?"

Mor tensed. She did not have to explain herself to the warrior, and yet she sensed that unless she spoke plainly, laid it all out before him, Tormud would not cease his attentions.

Leaning forward and placing her elbows upon the table, Mor met his gaze squarely. "Your looks and character do not move me in the slightest, Tormud. I have no wish to spend time with you, or to be touched by you."

Tormud held her gaze, his expression hardening. As she had hoped, her words had angered him. They were rude, although if she had so wished, she could have been ruder. There had been times over the years when she had been forced to rebuff men with her fists or a blade if the need be. She would not hesitate in this case either, if Tormud refused to heed her.

"You think you're too good for me, lass," he said finally, his voice a dangerous rumble. "But you aren't."

Mor shrugged, deliberately goading. "You've got that wrong. I simply don't want you. Is that so difficult to grasp?"

"A union between you and I could be advantageous to all," Tormud replied. A muscle bunched in his jaw, yet he was doing an admirable job of keeping his ire in check. "The Boar and The Serpent joined in marriage."

Mor's lip curled. "That mark on your arm is the only thing you have left of the people you forsook," she pointed out. "You are one of us now ... you have been for years. The Boar chieftain would slit your throat, before he would ever welcome you back into his tribe."

Tormud snorted. "Varar mac Urcal isn't so different to his father … he could be persuaded to welcome me back, if it meant an alliance between our peoples."

Silence fell between them. Mor frowned, pondering Tormud's words. They all knew things were not going well for The Serpent. Initially, when they had arrived upon these shores, the campaign had been a success. They had used the element of surprise, and their sheer numbers had crushed any resistance. The Boar stronghold of An Teanga was the first to fall to the invading Cruthini, but Varar mac Urcal had managed to take it back.

They now stood alone at Dun Ringill.

"The Boar chieftain isn't the loner you take him for," Mor said finally. "He stands with the other chieftains of this isle. He rode to their aid at Balintur, remember?"

The reminder caused Tormud's full lips to pucker up, as if he had tasted sour milk. Mor had just reminded him of the advice he had given Cathal earlier in the year: that The Boar would never willingly side with the other tribes of this isle. Her father had taken his word, and then shortly after An Teanga had fallen.

It was a sore subject for Tormud.

Resisting the urge to smile, Mor straightened up and drained the dregs of ale from her cup. It was getting late, and a pile of soft furs in her alcove beckoned. The bitter season was starting to drag on now. The chill weather had arrived just after Gateway and had not let up since. She longed for the soft warmth of a summer breeze, to feel the heat of the sun on her face, to inhale the woody scent of flowering heather. But spring still felt a long way off.

And spring was not something she could look forward to, for with it hostilities between her people and the other tribes would resume once more. Mor's breathing quickened at the thought. Her father was proud, but even he would have realized that after the siege of Balintur their numbers were seriously diminished. They could hold Dun Ringill for a time, for sure, but it was merely delaying the inevitable.

Mor glanced back toward the chieftain's table. Her father and uncle were still deep in intense discussion. Artair's scowl was now as fierce as Cathal's. She wondered if they were arguing that very subject.

Weariness spread through her, making Mor's shoulders sag a little.

It was the same sensation that had swept over her as she stood before that 'mother oak' a month earlier. She had grown so tired of conflict of late. For as long as Mor could remember, her people had fought against the neighboring tribes, until they finally drove them from their homeland. But arriving upon The Winged Isle had not brought the peace she had hoped for. Instead, the fighting here was much worse, much bloodier. They were now set on a course of destruction.

If her father did not change direction, they were all doomed.

"You're making a mistake shunning my affections." Tormud spoke up finally, shattering her introspection. There was no missing the threatening edge to his voice. "I'm not a man to forget such a slight ... you could do much worse than the likes of me."

His arrogance made Mor itch to lunge across the table and slam her fist into his nose. She was tired of this conversation and tired of him. She merely wanted to sink into her furs and forget about life for a short while. Instead, she gave him a cold look and inhaled deeply, preparing herself to utter the words that would end this discussion for good.

The crash of the heavy oaken door to the broch flying open and smashing against the wall prevented her.

Chapter Three

Captured

MOR TWISTED AROUND to see a tall, dark-haired man leap through the open doorway. In an instant, one of the warriors nearest the door leaped to his feet and tried to intercept him. An iron blade flashed, and The Serpent warrior crumpled.

As nimble as a running deer, the intruder dodged the next man to rush him and dove across the feasting hall. His gaze was upon the chieftain's table.

Upon her father.

A cry echoed through the hall as the intruder cut down another man who threw himself into his path. His pace did not slow, and his attention did not wander. He had wild eyes; his face twisted in a rictus of hate.

In a heartbeat, Mor was up.

She launched herself from her seat and tackled her father's would-be assassin, just four feet from the chieftain's table. In the meantime, neither Cathal nor Artair had moved. The attack had been so unexpected that both of them had frozen in surprise.

Mor and the intruder crashed to the rush-strewn floor, yet he twisted under her. His blade flashed, narrowly missing Mor's arm. She drove a knee into his gut and heard the air rush from his lungs.

Gripping hold of his right wrist, she yanked it back. However, his grip was as strong as iron, as was his arm. She gritted her teeth and threw her entire weight against him, struggling to hold the man still.

A heavy booted foot swung in then, catching the attacker on the side of the head.

Tormud had joined her.

The attacker grunted, falling back against the rushes. Mor took the opportunity to drive her knee into his belly once more. Then Tormud slammed his heavy foot down onto the attacker's wrist, grinding it into the floor till he released the warrior grip upon the blade.

But the attacker was not defeated yet. Cursing, his sea-blue eyes crazed with wrath, he kicked up, his knee driving into Mor's hip. She gritted her teeth against the pain and, drawing back her right arm, landed a hard punch on the intruder's cheek.

He spat out another curse, body arching up toward her as he got his left hand free and reached down to another blade that was strapped to his hip.

Mor slammed her knee down onto his hand, and as Tormud had done with his foot, ground the man's fingers into the floor.

Meanwhile, Tormud reached down, grabbed the intruder's head and smashed it against the floor— quelling the last of his struggles.

Talor hung limply in the warriors' arms, his head lolling while he struggled to keep conscious. His skull throbbed, as did his belly and chest. Darkness dimmed his vision, close to swallowing him—and yet he held on.

I've failed.

Bitterness coursed through him. He had done so well until the moment that bitch had thrown herself at him. Upon scaling the wall, he had loosed a volley of arrows, bringing down the warriors who guarded it, before he had crept down the slippery stone stairs into the village. It was late, and the snow still fell thickly, so most folk were indoors. Nonetheless, he had been forced to face the guards at the gates to the wall protecting the broch itself. Casting his bow and quiver of arrows aside, he had then drawn his sword and slashed his way through them.

After that, it had been just a few paces across the yard, up the steps, and into the broch.

He had spotted Calum mac Cathal immediately, sitting like some great red-haired cuckoo upon what was rightfully Galan mac Muin's chair. His uncle was chieftain of The Eagle. The Serpent chieftain had no business taking his place in this broch.

Breathing hard, Talor hung his head, awaiting the beating that would surely start. When it did not come, he glanced up, his blurred vision resting upon the tall auburn-haired man who stood a few feet away. The woman who had stopped him from reaching the chieftain's table stood next to Calum. One look at them standing next to each other—flame-haired and proud— and Talor realized that the woman who had thwarted him was Cathal's kin, most likely his daughter.

A heavyset warrior with short, greying dark hair stood close to Talor. That bastard had slammed his head into the floor so hard that Talor was surprised he had not cracked his skull like an egg.

Talor knew who the dark-haired warrior was though—he had seen him in battle. This was Tormud mac Alec—The Boar traitor.

Meeting his eye, Tormud favored Talor with a feral grin. He then swung his gaze over to Cathal. "Shall I beat him now?"

"Not yet," Cathal rumbled. He wore a harsh expression, and yet his moss-green eyes held a cunning gleam that made the first embers of fear spark within Talor. He did not like the calculating way The Serpent chieftain viewed him. "First, this Eagle warrior will tell me his name."

"Talor mac Donnel," Talor snarled. Of course, they had spied the mark of The Eagle tattooed onto his left bicep. "Nephew to The Eagle chieftain."

A slow smile spread across Cathal's face at this news. "Did Galan send you?"

Talor spat a gob of blood on to the ground at Cathal's feet. "No."

"So you have acted alone?"

"Obviously."

Cathal inclined his head, gaze narrowing slightly. "And why's that? You have the look of a man crazed by the need for vengeance."

Talor's lip curled. "You slew my sister at Balintur. I saw you."

Cathal stared back at him, his expression turning blank as he took this news in. And then, like watching a cloud move past the face of the sun, Talor saw recognition flare in Cathal's eyes. "I remember her," he said softly. "A young lass ... a pretty wee thing with braided hair." He paused here, smirking at Tormud while his daughter remained stone-faced, her green eyes narrowed as she never shifted her gaze from Talor. "She was vicious with that blade of hers ... but no match for me."

"Of course not," Tormud rumbled, while around them a few surrounding warriors laughed. Only Mor and the man still seated at the chieftain's table behind Cathal didn't share their mirth. The man seated was clearly kin to Cathal as well, although he had a rougher, more careworn face, his thinning auburn hair shaved close to his skull.

"So you came here to avenge her?" Cathal turned his attention back to Talor. The amusement on his face made Talor's belly cramp with rage. If two burly warriors had not been holding him fast, he would have launched himself at Cathal. He would have ripped his face off with his bare hands. The Serpent chieftain crossed heavily muscled arms across his broad chest. "Well, you have failed, and now I must decide what to do with you."

"That's easy," Tormud spoke up. "Kill him."

"All in good time," Cathal replied, his gaze never leaving Talor. "He'll be a feast for crows soon enough … but before he dies, Talor mac Donnel is going to tell us a few things about the army that is wintering at Balintur."

A heavy silence fell.

As the pain in his skull subsided slightly, Talor became aware of the sound of the crackling hearth behind him. The feasting hall was far busier than it had been when he entered. Folk had emerged from alcoves and gathered from the village beyond to set eyes on the man who had been foolish enough to try and slay their chieftain.

"Firstly," Cathal said, breaking the hush. "I wish to know how many of you there are. We slew many of the united tribes during the siege of Balintur. Tell me the number of those remaining."

A stony silence answered him.

Cathal inhaled deeply. "If you don't give me what I ask, the beating will be worse."

Talor did not answer. He merely stared back at Cathal, hatred clawing at his belly like a caged beast. They could beat him to death, it made no difference to him now. He would never betray his people.

"Looks like he's not going to talk," Tormud noted, cracking his knuckles as a bloodthirsty smile crept across his face. "Shall I loosen his tongue, chief?"

"Aye." Cathal stepped back, allowing the warrior to step forward. "Go on … enjoy yourself."

Mor watched the warrior slump, unconscious, in the arms of the two men holding him. His face was bloody. He had been handsome, before he had taken the beating, bearing finely chiseled features, startling blue eyes, a straight nose, and a sensual mouth. But those features were swollen, bruised, and bloodied now.

"He's stubborn," Tormud muttered, stepping back. The Boar warrior's face was red, and veins stood out on his neck. He had put a lot of effort into trying to make Talor mac Donnel talk, but the warrior had remained tight-lipped throughout. "Why don't you let me take him out into the snow and slit his throat?"

Beside Mor, her father heaved another sigh. "Because this man possesses details I need. He dies when I'm certain he won't talk … and not before."

Shifting her attention back to the unconscious man, Mor found herself sharing Tormud's opinion for once. The warrior was not going to talk. He was obstinate. The harder Tormud beat him, the more he clammed up.

"He's wasting all our time." Behind them, Artair spoke for the first time since the beating had begun. "Kill him, and be done with it."

Cathal cast his brother a look of thinly veiled irritation. "What's the hurry?"

Mor sensed the tension between them. Ever since the disaster at Balintur, the two brothers had argued far more than she had ever remembered. For years Artair had been content to follow his elder brother's lead. But now that they stood alone at Dun Ringill. Now that both Dunchadh and Tamhas, and many other valiant warriors, had fallen, Artair appeared to have developed strong opinions.

Turning his attention back to the unconscious Eagle warrior, Cathal's mouth thinned. "Chain him up to the wall. We'll question him again in the morning and see whether he's had a change of heart with the dawn."

Mor's mouth thinned. He would not.

Cathal then swung his gaze round, fixing Mor with a penetrating look. "You did well, daughter, bringing him down as you did."

"I had help," she murmured. As much as it galled her to admit it, she knew things might have gone ill for her if Tormud had not interceded. The Eagle warrior had fought with the wildness of a man who did not care if he lived or died. It had given him incredible strength. Without Tormud's help, he would likely have overpowered her eventually.

"Still." The corners of Cathal's mouth lifted. Ever since losing both his sons, he smiled rarely. But now there was warmth in his eyes. "You defended me without a thought to your own safety, lass ... I will not forget it."

Chapter Four

I'll Not Die a Traitor

MOR COULD NOT sleep.

Staring up at the darkness, she found herself reliving the events of the evening. Things had moved so fast she had not stopped to think. All she had known was that her father was in danger. And she'd had to protect him—no matter the cost.

Their prisoner was now chained up against the wall at the far end of the feasting hall, behind the raised platform where the chieftain's table sat. When she retired to her alcove, the man had still been unconscious. If he knew what was good for him, he would never awake.

Mor heaved an irritated sigh and closed her eyes. However, every time she tried to sleep, she saw Talor mac Donnel's bright blue gaze and remembered the way he had fearlessly faced down her father.

As angry as she had been that he had managed to breach their defenses and get so close to her father, Mor also fought a growing interest in the man. He was utterly fearless—almost to the point of madness. The warrior had come here for retribution for his slain sister, and although Mor would protect her own father with her last breath, she understood how he felt.

That familiar dull ache rose underneath her breast bone then, and she rolled over in her furs, trying to get comfortable. She had tried not to dwell too much on her brothers, but ever since Mid-Winter Fire, they were often on her mind. Their loss made her feel empty, as if the wind could blow right through her. Dunchadh and Tamhas were both very different men, and had not gotten along that well, yet she had been close to both of them.

In the two months following Tamhas's death, she had discovered loneliness: the sensation of feeling utterly alone in the world, even when she was surrounded by a hall of men and women. Without her brothers, she was adrift. She had not spoken of this to her father. Cathal would not understand. He was dealing with his own grief, his own loss. He did not need to share Mor's burden as well.

Mor huffed a sigh and rolled over onto her back once more. Before Talor mac Donnel had burst into the broch, she had been fighting tiredness. Even her altercation with Tormud had not been enough to keep her from needing sleep. Yet now, she felt wide awake.

Muttering a curse, Mor sat up and pushed the furs off. Naked, she got up and reached for her clothing: plaid breeches, a woolen tunic, and a fur-lined vest. Then, barefoot, she padded out of the alcove and into the sleeping hall.

All of the cressets, save those surrounding the prisoner, had been doused for the evening, casting most of the broch into shadowy darkness. However, the embers had not died in the hearth, and they emitted a soft ruddy glow over the lines of sleeping bodies spread out across the floor.

Fortunately, Mor would not have to disturb them in order to cross the hall, for a thin walkway circuited the space. A couple of feet wide, it ran around the edge before the curtained entrances to the many alcoves that lined the broch. Cathal, what remained of his kin, and his most trusted warriors slept in the alcoves. The rest of his people either slept on the floor inside the broch, or in one of the many stacked stone huts and roundhouses in the village outside.

Mor padded around the edge of the hall. On the way, she passed her father's alcove—the largest of those in the broch—and heard rumbling snores from within. A wry smile curved Mor's lips. Her father sounded like a sleeping dragon—he'd always snored, something his wife had complained much about over the years.

At the thought of her mother, Mor's step faltered. With everything that had happened of late, all the new losses that had drawn her attention, she sometimes went a day or two without thinking about her mother. And yet until recently, thoughts of her had dominated each waking moment. Lena had been her anchor; a formidable woman of great strength, it had been a shock to the whole tribe when she had succumbed to illness a year earlier.

Pushing aside thoughts of her mother, as the ache in her chest grew stronger, Mor resumed her path around the edge of the hall.

She came to a halt before the prisoner.

He sat upon his knees, arms stretched up either side of him. His breathing was slow and even, which made Mor suspect he was merely sleeping rather than unconscious.

Hunkering down, so that their gazes were level, she reached out and shook him by the shoulder.

Talor groaned, his long dark eyelashes fluttering against his cheeks. Not for the first time, Mor was struck by the beauty of his face. Even swollen and bruised, it drew her eye and aroused a strange fascination within her.

She gently shook him once more, and slowly, his eyes opened. The prisoner then lifted his chin, and their gazes fused.

Mor inhaled sharply, and for a long moment the pair of them merely stared at each other. The air inside the broch was chill, now that the hearth had died down, but heat seeped through Mor's limbs nonetheless. She felt as if she were standing before a roaring fire. Her breathing quickened, and the moment drew out. And yet neither of them spoke.

Eventually though, it was Mor who broke the silence between them. "Da should have killed you tonight." Her voice was soft, barely above a whisper.

His mouth quirked. Despite that he was beaten and in chains, this man's arrogance reached out, enveloping her. "Have you come to do what he wouldn't then?"

"No ... I've come to warn you. Give him what he wants tomorrow, or your end will be a painful one."

Talor mac Donnel huffed a bitter laugh. "What do I care?" he rasped. "I'll not die a traitor."

Mor watched him, drinking in the haughty lines of his face. She liked the rough timbre of his voice, the sultry lilt of his accent—different to her own flatter tones.

"You don't fear pain then?" she asked coolly. She was not sure why she had gotten up in the middle of the night to speak to this man. It was almost as if an invisible hand had taken hers and led her here; she felt compelled to converse with him.

Again, that arrogant half-smile. His blue eyes gleamed in the light of the nearby cressets. "Not half as much as failure."

"But you *have* failed."

His mouth twisted. "Aye, thanks to you."

"I wasn't going to let you cut my father down, was I?"

"He's a butcher."

"We're all butchers, mac Donnel. How many warriors have you slain in the heat of battle?"

Talor's gaze guttered, and Mor realized that finally, she had gotten to him, had managed to penetrate his brash shield.

"I didn't invade your home," he replied after a moment, his voice harsh now. "I didn't take lands that were not my own."

"My father says land belongs to no one. The strongest take what they want ... it's always been that way."

His lip curled. "What's your name?"

"Mor."

"Mor." A shiver of pleasure went through her as he said her name, even if wrath burned in his eyes now. His swollen face had gone taut and strained. "You can take what you want, but that doesn't mean you get to keep it."

The threatening edge to his voice did not intimidate her. Instead, it sent a frisson of excitement through her lower belly, igniting a fire there that had lain dormant for months now. Back on the mainland she had taken a lover, but their relationship had ended before the invasion. The warrior had fallen during the initial conflict with The Boar—and after that she had been too preoccupied with war to think about taking another consort.

It surprised her that this prisoner, this local man who had been about to slay her father, incited such a response.

Likewise, she saw his pupils dilate as he stared back at her. He felt it too—this unsettling pull.

"I suggest," Mor said after a long pause, "that you cooperate with my father tomorrow. Give him details, false ones if you want ... and he may give you a warrior's death."

Talor watched the woman with fiery auburn hair and moss-green eyes. He did not understand why she had approached him, or even why she was bothering to give him advice. Yet the longer they talked, the more he wanted her to stay.

The impact of their gazes meeting had hit him like a blow to the belly. Even now, he reeled in the aftermath, and was at a loss as to why he had reacted so strongly. He had fought her earlier in the hall, and she had watched while her father's men beat him.

But now, face-to-face, while the rest of the keep slumbered, something sparked.

She observed him with cool appraisal, and during the silences between them, he noted her reaction to his closeness: the way her breathing quickened, the parting of her full lips.

He had never seen a woman like this one.

She was taller than any woman of his tribe, tall enough to stand eye-to-eye with him. Broad-shouldered and full-breasted, she had long limbs and narrow hips. But it was her face he could not take his eyes off. She had high cheekbones, milky skin, and a scattering of freckles across the bridge of her nose. She crouched so close that he could smell the sweet, musky scent of her skin.

And despite everything, despite that his body ached and that he could no longer feel his hands, his groin tightened. He resolutely ignored the arousal; it had poor timing indeed.

"You said nothing earlier," he murmured finally, breaking the tension-filled silence between them. "Why?"

Those full lips curved. "I prefer to let my father interrogate prisoners without interference," she replied. Mor had a beguiling voice, low and sultry. "He knows what he's doing."

"And yet you're here … giving me advice on how to deal with him. Why?"

Again, that cool smile, although her gaze was now shadowed. "Grief sent you on this mission … it was a stupid, yet noble reason. You're reckless and clearly half-mad to break into this fort on your own. But I respect you for your actions. I know what grief can do to someone."

Chapter Five

Games

DESPITE THAT HE had told himself he would not listen to the woman, Talor decided to take Mor's advice the following day.

He had hung there, awake and in pain, for a long while after she left him. Talor had watched her walk away, noting her long, confident strides, her proud bearing, and the way her wild auburn hair tumbled down her back.

The Mother save him, he did not want to lust after this Serpent woman, and yet his shaft had gone rock hard as his gaze traveled down the length of her to where those plaid breeches hugged the contours of her rounded buttocks.

Lust. It was just lust. He had not lain with a woman in a while. Ever since Bonnie's death, he had no longer felt like flirting or enjoying female company as he used to. Usually, every fire festival was an opportunity to find a woman to warm his furs for a night or two. But at Mid-Winter Fire, he had taken the watch upon the walls of

Balintur while his friends and family celebrated the Long Night.

This was probably his last night alive, and as he watched Mor walk away, he wished he could have spent it in her furs, driving into her as she wrapped those long legs about him. She was the enemy, but he wanted her nonetheless.

By the time dawn arrived, Talor had fallen into a pain-filled doze, all lusty thoughts gone. His whole body throbbed now, the parts of it he could actually feel. And when they released him from the wall, he merely crumpled to the floor, unable to support himself with his arms or legs.

The Cruthini dogs who had cut him down laughed long and hard at that. One of them got in a sharp kick to his ribs for good measure, before Cathal's piercing reprimand brought them up short.

"Hands off," The Serpent chieftain barked. "Give the prisoner bread and broth. I don't want him fainting, before I get a chance to question him."

Talor sat, back pressed up against the wall, rubbing his tingling wrists as a Cruthini woman brought him a bowl of broth and a hunk of oaten bread. She shoved them at him, her expression as hard as her eyes.

Unlike Mor, this one was no beauty.

Lifting the bowl to his lips, Talor took a gulp, sighing as the hot liquid filled his belly. He had not eaten since leaving Balintur. He had been in such pain that he had barely noticed the hunger gnawing at his belly.

He lowered the bowl and set it on the floor beside him, before tearing off a piece of bread and stuffing it into his mouth. He spied the chieftain's daughter then. She was seated a few yards away at her father's table.

She did not look his way.

However, that Boar traitor, Tormud, was glaring at him from the far end of the table. He had been frustrated the night before, itching to take Talor outside and spill his entrails onto the snow. He would be hoping for the chance this morning.

Revived by the food and drink, Talor leaned back against the wall. Never had he been so relieved to have the chance to simply sit. Hanging there by his arms all night had made them feel as if they were slowly being pulled from their sockets.

Breathing deeply, Talor closed his eyes. Exhaustion settled over him in a heavy mantle, turning his thoughts foggy and his emotions jumbled. Through it all though, he knew he was a doomed man.

The chieftain's daughter's words echoed in his head as he dozed against the wall.

Give him details, false ones if you want … and he may give you a warrior's death.

Cathal was desperate, Talor had seen it in his eyes the night before. Talor did not care how he died—the result would be just the same in the end. But stubbornness would not aid him now. There was always a chance Cathal might free him from his chains, might give him the chance to attack him again.

And this time Talor would not fail.

Excitement tightened his breathing at the thought.

He had come here to avenge Bonnie, but instead had ended up a prisoner. If he got another chance, he would not fail again.

Cathal mac Calum took his time over his oatcakes and ale. He ate a mountain of oatcakes, slathering them with butter and honey. And despite that the broth and bread had taken the edge off Talor's hunger, his belly growled nonetheless.

Talor's mouth thinned. His stomach did not seem to realize that he would not likely live to see another dawn.

Mor broke her fast in silence, her gaze never once straying to Talor.

He could almost believe she had not visited him in the night—but he could not forget the heat that had flared between them.

Finishing his last oatcake, Cathal brushed crumbs off his broad chest and shifted his gaze to Talor.

"Are you ready to talk now?"

Talor stared back at him, keeping his stubborn silence. It was best not to look too helpful, or the chieftain would suspect he was being played.

Cathal cast a sidelong glance at his brother. Artair lifted his cup of ale to his lips with a shrug. "I did warn you," he replied.

Cathal huffed out a breath and rose to his feet. Seated on the ground, Talor was forced to raise his chin to meet the man's eye. He was huge, frankly, the biggest man that Talor had ever set eyes upon. What did these Cruthini eat as bairns that made them grow so tall and strong?

"Get him on his feet," Cathal ordered, and two warriors—the same two who had held Talor while he was beaten the night before—rose from the table below the platform and made their way over to him.

Talor heaved out a weary sigh. The reprieve had been too short.

The warriors hauled him to his feet, and Talor clenched his jaw to prevent himself from crying out. Pain lanced across his chest, and he imagined that under his vest, his torso would be mottled with bruises.

"Very well, Eagle. Let's start again." Cathal moved closer to him. "Tell me of the numbers at Balintur."

Talor held his silence and braced himself for the blow that would follow. The heavy punch to the guts made him double over as pain pulsed through him. He wanted to hold his tongue, to let them beat him to death if need be, but he remembered his resolve. Let him play with Cathal a while.

"Just under three hundred warriors," he wheezed.

Silence followed this proclamation, and when Cathal spoke, his voice was rough with suspicion. "That seems too few."

It was. There were nearer four hundred warriors camped at Balintur.

"Many died during the siege," Talor replied, his voice raspy as he struggled to catch his breath. The punch to the belly made him feel sick. One more blow like that and he would throw up the broth and bread he had recently consumed. "Some perished from their wounds afterward as well."

A brittle silence fell. Talor watched Cathal's face. He was viewing Talor with a narrow-eyed stare that made Talor realize The Serpent chieftain was no fool.

"Three hundred warriors it is then," he replied, his voice was soft but held an edge of menace to it nonetheless. "Let's hear you answer another question."

Talor held his gaze, injecting a dose of belligerence into his own.

"Who holds the most influence of the four chieftains?" Cathal asked after a pause.

Talor pretended to consider this. The truth was that he had not seen any of the four dominate the others. Galan and Varar had led some of the campaigns merely because they were on their lands, but they did not hold sway over the other chieftains. However, he would not tell Cathal that. "Galan mac Muin of The Eagle," he said. "My uncle is not a man to cross."

"And yet he rode away from Dun Ringill without a backward glance," Tormud spoke up, his tone goading. "That isn't the act of a fearless leader."

Rage surged, cramping Talor's belly. Tormud's insult had cut deep; like all The Eagle warriors, Talor had hated leaving Dun Ringill. Initially, he had questioned his uncle's decision to abandon the fort. Later though, he had understood the wisdom in it. At that stage the invaders had far outnumbered them. Galan had been right: they were far stronger united with the other tribes.

"Traitor," Talor snarled out the word as he met Tormud's eye. "Your opinion isn't worth shit to me."

Tormud smirked, although Talor saw anger flare in the man's eyes. He had hit a nerve.

"And who is the weak link?" Cathal pushed on. "Who among the chieftains would be most likely to betray the others?"

Talor hesitated at this question. He did not like the way Cathal's mind worked. He was as cunning as a weasel. He was looking for something to exploit. Once again, Talor did not see any of the chieftains as capable of betraying the others. Even Wid of The Wolf—who had argued with the others over some of the decisions—was committed to ridding the isle of this scourge. But he would not reveal that to Cathal. He would let him believe one of them could be brought to his side.

"Varar mac Urcal," he said after a lengthy pause. His gaze then returned to Tormud. "A Boar cannot be trusted."

It had not been so long ago that Talor would have believed such an accusation. Relations between The Eagle and The Boar had been strained over the years, with many bloody altercations in their history. But Talor respected Varar. The Boar chieftain, though he could be even more arrogant than Talor himself at times, had proved himself worthy of trust. He had also won Talor's cousin, Fina's, heart.

Tormud screwed up his face. "He lies."

"Everyone on this isle knows that The Boar are loners. They prefer to keep their own counsel," Talor continued, ignoring Tormud's outburst. "Varar mac Urcal cares not for the fate of the other tribes. He has returned to An Teanga and will remain there."

"So, he will not aid the rest of you to take back Dun Ringill?" Cathal did not bother to hide the skepticism in his voice.

Talor snorted. "He says he will ... but I doubt his word. So do many others."

A heavy silence followed this proclamation. Talor held his tongue, wondering if he had said too much. None of the surrounding warriors looked happy. Both Cathal's brother and Mor, still seated at the chieftain's table, were frowning.

Talor wondered if Cathal's daughter realized he was bluffing. Recklessness flooded through him in a hot tide. He was starting to enjoy this. He had always been clever with words and wondered if he could manage to tie these Cruthini up in knots. If he filled their heads with nonsense, The Serpent might make a critical mistake, one that could result in their downfall.

The silence drew out, and then Cathal mac Calum's face went stony, his gaze shuttering. He stepped back from Talor and shifted his attention to Tormud. "We're done here. Beat him unconscious, and then hang him up by his arms outside the broch walls." Cathal's gaze returned to Talor, a wolfish smile stretching across his features. Talor understood then that the chieftain had not been fooled—not for a moment. "The cold can do the rest."

Chapter Six

Standing Together

MUIN MAC GALAN walked into the meeting house, shaking the snow off his cloak. The others had already arrived and were seated around the glowing firepit. The roar of agitated voices hit Muin in a wave, as did the odor of wet wool and leather.

"There you are, Muin!" His mother, Tea, waved him over to where his kin had gathered at one edge of the fire. His father, Galan, wore a grim expression as he discussed something urgently with his brother Donnel.

Muin hesitated, noting his uncle's austere face. He then nodded to his mother and crossed to the place she had kept for him, between her and his younger brother, Aaron.

"I can't believe he's done this," Aaron growled, before he shot Muin an accusing look. "Did you suspect he would?"

Muin frowned. "You think I knew?"

"Talor is closer to you than anyone. If he was going to share his plans, it would be with you."

Muin sighed. Of course, Talor would not have confided in Aaron. The two cousins argued often of late. Both young men were too strong-willed, too cocky, to be friends. In contrast, Muin and Talor had always been as close as brothers. Even if they had not been cousins, the pair of them would have been firm friends. Their characters complemented each other: Muin was quiet and steady, while Talor was forthright and impulsive.

Muin's frown deepened. He had never minded his cousin's reckless nature till now, but he had taken things too far this time.

"He said nothing to me," Muin replied. "You know he hasn't been himself of late. Ever since Bonnie died, Talor has closed up. He's been avoiding me ... I was one of the last to know he'd gone missing."

A pang of guilt needled Muin then. He had been so happy in his new life with Ailene he had noticed little else. He knew his cousin was miserable. Talor's brooding manner and strange silences had worried him, but he had not perhaps paid enough attention. Ailene had become his world, and after so many years of yearning for what he thought he could never have, he had reveled in it. They had been handfasted just days earlier, the happiest moment of Muin's life.

"We must send warriors after him," a rough, angry voice cut through the din.

Donnel, Talor's father, had spoken.

The tall, dark-haired warrior rose to his feet, an act that caused the chatter around the fireside to die away. One look at his uncle's face, and Muin knew why he had once been named the 'Battle Eagle'. His slate-grey gaze blazed, and a muscle flexed in his chiseled jaw. Even now, in his mid-forties, Donnel mac Muin was not a warrior to underestimate. Watching him, Muin reflected how similar Donnel and Talor were, not just in looks—although it was clear from one glance that Talor was Donnel's son—but in character too.

Galan had told Muin how, as a younger man, Donnel had been restless and reckless; he had gone savage with grief after the loss of his first wife, Luana.

"There is little point in sending warriors after Talor, Donnel ... you must realize that." Wid mac Manus, chieftain of The Wolf, was the first to answer him. A dark-haired, stocky, bearded man of a similar age to Donnel, Wid bore a careworn face. "You know as well as I that they will have him by now. If by some miracle he managed to bring Cathal down, he won't have escaped the broch alive."

Wid's words were direct, harsh even. Rage pulsed through Muin at the thought of his cousin falling into Serpent hands, but he would not lose hope that his cousin still lived—not yet.

Muin watched Donnel stare Wid down. The glower on his uncle's face told him that he too was not ready to accept Wid's grim view of the situation.

"I won't leave him there," Donnel ground out the words. "I will go and bring back my son's body alone, if I have to."

"You know it won't come to that." Tarl, who had been seated next to Donnel, spoke up. The middle of the three brothers, Tarl mac Muin wore a strained expression this morning, although his grey eyes were as hard as Donnel's. "One thing's for sure though ... Talor's departure changes our plans."

"How so?" Tadhg mac Fortrenn, chieftain of The Stag, spoke up. The only chieftain not present this morning was Varar of The Boar. He and Muin's cousin, Fina, had departed for An Teanga, The Boar stronghold, after Muin and Ailene's handfasting a few days earlier.

"We were going to attack anyway," Tarl replied, meeting Tadhg's eye. "After the snows had cleared." Tarl's jaw hardened then. "But now we can't wait. We must hit them now ... and hard."

Aggression surged in a hot tide through Muin's veins. It was similar to the sensation that rose within him in battle—a type of madness that seized him and made him lose all fear for his own safety. Like his uncles, he had no intention of sitting on his hands while Talor died in Serpent hands.

A charged silence settled over the meeting house.

Galan met Tadhg's gaze for a long moment, before he shifted his attention to Wid. "Naturally, I agree with my brothers," he murmured. "I wish to move on Dun Ringill at our first opportunity. What say you both? Will you join us?"

The silence continued. Wid and Tadhg shared a long look. There was no aggression on either of their faces, just weary resignation. They had both agreed to help take back Dun Ringill moons ago. They were assisting The Eagle, but they were also helping themselves. Once Dun Ringill fell, the hold that The Serpent had over The Winged Isle would shatter. They could return home to their brochs knowing that these invading Cruthini no longer posed a threat.

"Very well," Wid said finally, "The Wolf is with you."

"As is The Stag ... although the snow will make the siege harder on us," Tadhg pointed out. He was a huge, broad-shouldered man and this morning wore his ceremonial cloak, which bore the head and antlers of a great red stag. It made The Stag chieftain an imposing sight indeed. "But I can see why you wish to attack now. Talor may yet still breathe."

"And if he doesn't, I'll slaughter every last one of those Cruthini bastards to avenge him," Donnel's growled threat split the air.

The fire in Muin's belly raged hotter still. They were fighting words. His churning worry for Talor morphed into something fierce and dark. He had to believe his cousin still lived, but if he discovered otherwise, he would bring down any Serpent who crossed his path.

"I will send out riders to An Teanga immediately," Galan broke the tension-filled silence that filled the meeting house. "Varar has vowed to stand with us. He and Fina can meet us east of the fort."

The other two chieftains nodded at this. They knew that Varar mac Urcal had pledged to fight alongside them, although his oath had surprised them.

Muin was not surprised though. He had no doubts about Varar, not any longer. He had fought alongside the man enough times of late to know that his word was good. Plus, he was wed to Fina, Tarl's fiery daughter. The Boar and The Eagle were now united in marriage—an alliance that would strengthen both tribes.

Together, the united tribes of The Winged Isle would stand against The Serpent.

Muin emerged from the meeting roundhouse to find that a blizzard had blown in. The snow fell in heavy, swirling flakes, nearly blinding him.

Behind him Aaron cursed as he stepped out into the calf-deep snow. "How are we supposed to go to battle in this weather?" he muttered.

Muin cut his brother a sharp look. "We'll manage," he replied. "We need to move now, Aaron. Perhaps if we do, there's a chance that Talor still lives."

His brother's gaze guttered then, and Muin realized that despite Aaron's bluster, he was genuinely worried about Talor. The two of them bickered constantly, although even that had ceased of late as Talor closed himself off from friends and family. But there was real affection underneath—just like Talor, Aaron had a good heart.

The two brothers trudged through the snow, making their way through a warren of narrow streets back to the hut where Muin lived with Ailene. The roundhouse that Aaron shared with his parents lay farther down the street, but Muin motioned for his brother to follow him. "Ailene is preparing stew and dumplings for the noon meal," Muin told him with a half-smile. "There's plenty for you too ... if you're hungry?"

It was a foolish question. Aaron was always hungry. Even so, his brother hesitated a moment before nodding. He did not like to interrupt upon Muin and Ailene's time alone.

"Are you sure?"

"Aye ... Ailene always cooks too much. You know that."

Aaron grinned. "Watch out, brother, or you'll run to fat."

Ducking into the hut, both men stamped the snow off their boots on the front step and did their best to remove their snow encrusted cloaks without showering the interior of the dwelling with snowflakes.

"Close the door … quickly," a female voice instructed. "That wind is freezing."

Muin hastily did as bid before following his brother to the fireside. A tall, dark-haired woman with sea-blue eyes stood over a bubbling cauldron of stew. Her cheeks were flushed; it was hot inside the hut, in sharp contrast to the bitter wind outdoors.

At the sight of his wife, the rage and urgency within Muin dimmed a little. Ailene, who was the bandruí—seer—of The Eagle tribe, was his anchor in an increasingly uncertain world.

Ailene's gaze met his, and a knowing look flared in her eyes. She had been surprised when the chieftains had not called her with Muin to the meeting. As seer, she was usually requested to join them for such gatherings.

"You're going after him, aren't you?" she asked.

"Aye," Muin replied gruffly as he warmed his hands before the fire. "We're going to launch our campaign early against Dun Ringill."

Ailene's gaze widened. "When?"

"As soon as we are ready."

His wife's slender jaw tensed. "I should have been at the meeting. Didn't they want me to cast the bones?"

Muin tensed. Of course, his people rarely went to war without consulting their bandruí first. However, there had been conflict between Ailene and the chieftains before Mid-Winter Fire. Ailene had made a mistake that nearly cost them all dearly. Muin wondered if the chieftains had deliberately not requested Ailene's presence at the meeting—perhaps Wid and Tadhg still sought to punish her. "There will be time for that, love," he replied. "We will need you to bless the warriors, before we move out."

Ailene's mouth compressed. "And if I cast the bones and see something worrying?"

Next to Muin, Aaron shifted uncomfortably on his seat. "I thought your tellings have been more positive of late," Muin's brother replied with a frown.

She nodded. "I cast the bones on the eve of the Long Night and saw a far brighter future for our people."

"Aye," Muin murmured, meeting his wife's eye across the fire. "No longer does a cloud of doom hang over us … it's the right time to move."

"And what of my prediction that The Eagle and The Serpent will somehow be united in the future?"

Ailene's words brought a derisive snort from Aaron, and although Muin cut him a quelling look, he found himself agreeing with his brother. He could not see a day when such a thing would ever come to pass.

"Maybe, this is one of the rare instances when the bones are wrong, mo ghràdh," he replied.

Chapter Seven

Worse Ways to Die

THERE WERE WORSE ways to die.

They could have slit open his belly, pulled out his entrails, and left him to fade in slow agony. Instead, Cathal had decided to let Talor gradually freeze as he hung from the outer wall of Dun Ringill. It was a kinder death than he had expected—but the end result would be the same.

The day was waning. It was snowing so heavily that Talor had not been able to track the progress of the sun across the sky. But even through the surrounding curtain of white, he realized that the light was dimming.

Soon night would be upon them, and the temperature would plummet. Already, he could not feel his hands or feet. The cold cocooned him, strangely removing a lot of the aches and pains the beatings had caused.

Talor knew that was not a good sign. It meant his body was slowly shutting down. And he knew when he ceased to feel the cold at all, the end would be near. He had seen men freeze to death before. They had stopped shivering and even complained of being too warm.

Idiot.

He had not thought his attack through at all. Blinded by revenge, an illness that had raged through him for the past two moons, Talor had been unable to think of anything else.

He had just wanted Cathal dead. And he had wanted to be the one to drive his blade into the bastard's throat.

But it had all gone awry. Bonnie would not be avenged. And soon he would be joining her in the halls of their fathers.

Despair filtered through Talor then. He did not recognize it at first, the heavy numbing sensation that dragged down at him, penetrating the chills that wracked his body. As The Reaper approached, his gleaming scythe at the ready, it dawned on Talor that he had perhaps been a trifle careless to throw his life away.

Suddenly, he wanted nothing more than to live.

He thought then of all the things he would miss. He would never see another spring bloom, would not see the world come to life after the bleakness of the bitter season. He would never warm himself again by a roaring fire.

He would never lie with a woman again, or down a horn of mead, or eat a dish of blood sausage.

The despair grew heavier still, like a boulder fastened around his neck.

Survival had not mattered to him of late. Life had become a struggle, and he had been filled with rage that no one else seemed to care as much as he did that Bonnie was gone. He had felt bitterness toward his father and Eithni—that they still continued with their lives.

The world should have stopped, and yet it hadn't.

He now knew better—now when it was too late to do anything about it.

Life and death were just part of the same cycle, and fighting against it was futile. All he had done was shorten his own life in this reckless pursuit of vengeance.

Bonnie wouldn't care. Bonnie was gone.

"Lackwit," he muttered to himself. "You deserve this end."

"What's that?" A Serpent warrior, bundled up in furs, who was standing guard a few feet away, called out. "Did you just squawk, Eagle?"

"I was just wondering if you'd cut me down and sit me in front of a warm fire with a dish of hot stew?" Talor called back. "It's a little chilly out here."

The warrior snorted. "No chance of that. I'd use your imagination if I were you," he replied gruffly. "Remember your last meal fondly ... because you won't be getting another."

"Do you think he's dead yet?" Tormud's question rumbled across the table, causing some of the warriors seated around him to chortle.

"I don't know," Artair replied, raising a dark eyebrow at the warrior. "You could brave the blizzard and check for yourself?"

"I don't think I'll bother," Tormud replied with a sneer. "It's cold out there."

More laughter followed this comment. Looking on, Mor noted just how much sway Tormud held here. Obviously, the warriors of their tribe followed Cathal and none other, but at the same time many of them held a deep respect for Tormud. He was a man who knew how to command and inspired respect in those who fought alongside him. However, Mor, like Tamhas, had never shared their respect.

Tormud raised his cup to his lips and took a deep draft of mead. Then his attention shifted to where Cathal sat in his high-backed wooden chair, drinking horn in hand. "I still think you should have let me have some more fun with Talor mac Donnel," The Boar warrior muttered. "Freezing to death is too kind for the likes of him."

Cathal shrugged. "Either way, he'll be dead by morning."

Mor studied her father's face and wondered at his thoughts. She had advised Talor to break his silence, but he had taken it too far earlier, giving details that her father had suspected were false. Not surprisingly, Cathal had seen through him.

Mor sat at the far end of the table, an untouched cup of mead before her. They had just consumed a light supper of turnip and cabbage stew, accompanied by cheese curd dumplings. But Mor had eaten little. She'd had a poor appetite all day, and had felt on edge—restless inside the confines of the broch.

Underneath the table her foot tapped restively. She often felt like this in winter, confined by the snow and cold weather. But today was worse. After the events of the night before, she did not feel herself.

She appreciated that her father had not been unnecessarily cruel to the Eagle warrior. Nonetheless, the thought of Talor slowly freezing to death outside in that biting wind put her on edge.

The sensation irritated her.

She did not know the man and had every reason to despise him. And yet she was irresistibly drawn to him. She was not sure what had caused her to rise from her furs and go to speak with him, but once she had, their brief conversation had plagued her for the rest of the night. She had deliberately remained aloof from Talor the following morning, but it did not matter. A tenuous link had been somehow forged between them.

This fierce, reckless stranger, who seemed to care so little for his own life, had brought all the things that had been churning within her for a while now to a head.

His presence here only made her feelings plainer.

She wanted an end to war, an end to this invasion.

Mor was not afraid of a fight, or of falling in a bloody battle, but she was tired of the struggle. She was tired of rising every morning ready to fight yet again. The conflict that she had grown up with had followed them to The Winged Isle, and it would never end.

"I see you and uncle often discussing things, Da," she said finally, speaking up for the first time that evening. "Do you speak of the future?"

Cathal snorted. "We *argue* about the future, lass, if that's what you mean."

A few feet away, Artair grimaced.

"And why's that?" Mor asked.

"Our time here is coming to an end," Artair replied, ignoring the dark glance that his older brother cast him. Her uncle sat hunched over his cup of mead. The cold made his healing injuries pain him. "I believe that we would be wise to pack up and leave The Winged Isle, before the warriors of the united tribes come for us."

Mor's heart leaped at the suggestion. Her uncle had been bold to argue for such a thing.

"That is the act of a coward," Cathal growled.

Anger lit in Artair's eyes. "It's not craven to look after your people," he pointed out. "If things continue as they are, every last Serpent upon this rock will die. Is that what you want?"

"Our chieftain speaks true," Tormud spoke up, casting Artair a sneering look. "There can be no turning back, no retreat."

Silence fell over the table, and despite that it was warm inside the feasting hall, a chill settled over Mor. She agreed with her uncle, if they kept to their current course, only death and destruction would follow. She was not surprised that Tormud refused to back down. The man felt he had a claim to the lands here—but not so her father. Cathal was born and bred on the mainland, and his roots were there. He had made a mistake in coming here, they all had. But stubbornness had overtaken him of late, perhaps as a result of his grief.

"Unlike Artair, I don't think we should flee," she said finally, only to earn a scowl from her uncle. But Mor pressed on. "Instead, we should make peace with the tribes of this isle."

It was rare for her to voice an opinion contrary to her father's, and she saw surprise ripple across his face. Tamhas had always been the one to lock horns with him. Until now she had only ever sought to gain her father's praise, not risk his ire.

Cathal's brow furrowed. "What's this?" he growled. "Has my fierce daughter lost her stomach for war?"

"I've never loved war for the sake of it," she replied, keeping her voice cool to mask the anger that was now simmering in her gut. "I followed you here because I thought we were going to a better life. But the only things I have known on this isle are grief and loss. If we want a new life in this place, we need to work with the people here, not against them."

Her father glowered back at her. "A Serpent doesn't share power, girl." His voice turned flint-hard, and his green eyes darkened as his temper rose. "When I led us across the water to this isle, I knew there would be bloodshed. I brought us here ... and I will see us to victory. No matter what it takes."

Mor stepped up onto the walls and breathed in, drawing in a great lungful of gelid air.

She had come up here to think, but the steps leading up to the top of the wall had been perilous, even for one as light footed as her. It was not her turn to take the night watch; she should not even be up here.

Peering through the fluttering snow, Mor could see the huddled, cloaked figures of warriors farther up the wall, their hunched shoulders outlined against the burning braziers that ringed the walls of the fort. One or two of the faces she glimpsed were pale and strained. Like many within these walls, they wore worried expressions, hope for the future leeching from them.

One of the men peered at her curiously, but Mor ignored him. Apart from her alcove, this was one of the few places where she could be alone. She needed to think.

Something was building inside her, a sensation that had been flowering for a while now.

She had not liked it at first. When the traitorous thoughts had first presented themselves on the eve of the Long Night, she had tried not to dwell upon them. But even before the reckless Talor mac Donnel had burst into her life, she had been considering going against her father to achieve peace. She had even entertained the idea of riding to Balintur and offering herself up to the enemy as a gesture of goodwill.

A healthy sense of self-preservation had prevented her. If she took that road, there would be no returning from it.

Mor walked to the edge of the wall, her boots sinking into the ankle-deep snow, and stared out at the murky horizon. She knew Loch Slapin lay before her, but she could barely make it out, for the blizzard had closed in, enclosing her in a bleak, white world.

Night was falling. The prisoner would not last much longer—if he had not perished already.

The conflict within her surged, clamping her ribs in a vise and making it hard to breathe.

Mor balled her hands into fists and drew in another deep breath.

She had not wanted the situation to come to this. She hated the idea of being pitted against her father. But the conversation after supper had proved to her what she had suspected for a while now. Cathal mac Calum's desire to control this isle had turned into madness. He could not see clearly any more. He could not seem to make a rational decision. To an onlooker, the situation was hopeless. Her uncle had been attempting in vain for days now to sway his brother's opinion.

But Tormud was always there, whispering into her father's ear. This was Tormud's homeland, and it had become evident of late that the warrior wished to remain on The Winged Isle, to put down roots here again. Mor could not help but think that The Boar warrior was using her father to his own ends. But Cathal was too proud to see it.

Mor let out a long breath, watching it cloud in the icy air before her. This was it—the turning point had come.

She had to act tonight, or not at all.

Chapter Eight

Not Dead Yet

TALOR COULD NOT feel his body any longer. The numbness had started in his lower limbs and worked its way up into his torso. And as night fell, he wondered how long it would be, before the cold ended him.

Part of him hoped it would be swift, for this was not a warrior's death. The best end he could have chosen was death in battle, like Bonnie. Instead, he had been chained to the wall of his own broch, and now hung there limply.

Closing his eyes, Talor whispered a prayer to The Hag, the goddess that presided over the bitter season. She would be waiting nearby in the shadow of the god of death, The Reaper.

This isn't my time. It seemed a bit foolish to think such a thing. Death came when it chose to. However, in his gut, Talor knew that this was not his moment. This was not how he was supposed to die.

An image of his father floated before him then. Donnel mac Muin's proud face, with his grey eyes that could go as hard as iron when angered and the color of a stormy sky when he laughed. They had clashed increasingly often of late. It was not anything unusual; even Muin, who was far less argumentative than Talor, had locked horns with his own father in the past year. Even so, now that he would never see Donnel again, Talor wished he had not been so stubborn, so determined to carve his own path. There had been times over the past year or so when he had deliberately shunned his father's well-meant advice.

He had not wanted his old man to tell him what to do. It seemed so petty now.

Sagging against the iron manacles that bit into his wrists, Talor's chin dropped toward his chest.

Sorry, Da. How he wished he could go back in time and do things differently.

"Mac Donnel," a cool female voice intruded upon his self-pity. "You're not dead yet?"

Talor's eyes fluttered open, surprise filtering through him when his gaze rested upon the chieftain's daughter.

Mor stood before Talor, swathed in furs. Her gaze narrowed as she surveyed him.

Talor swallowed. He had barely the strength to respond to her. Yet he managed to dredge up the words. "Come to gloat, have you?" he rasped. "I took your advice, and look where it got me."

"I told you to speak to my father," she replied with a frown. "Not to take him for a fool. You're lucky he didn't gut you then and there."

If Talor had been able to shrug, he would have. Frankly, Cathal would have done him a kindness to save him this pitiful end.

"I'm not here to gloat," Mor said when he did not answer.

Talor glanced left to right, realizing then that they stood alone. The glow of a nearby brazier usually illuminated the cloaked outlines of guards that had watched over him all day. But they were now absent.

"I'm here to make you an offer," Mor continued. "Think carefully upon it, for I won't ask twice."

Talor stared back at her. He was so cold that he could not bring himself to care about any offer she could make him. Nonetheless, he eventually replied, "Go on."

"I will free you and take you from Dun Ringill," she said softly, stepping closer to him. In the flickering light of the brazier, her eyes had deepened to a deep jade green. "But in return, you must swear an oath that you will cease your quest for vengeance against my father. You must swear that you will do as I ask, and follow me."

For a moment or two her request did not register.

Was this woman actually offering to free him? It made no sense at all.

"Why would you do that?" The question came out in a croak.

A nerve flickered on her cheek, and the woman frowned. A moment later she drew in a steadying breath, casting another cautious look from side to side before answering him. "I'm tired to my bones of this war," she murmured. "Our people won't survive the coming year, and yet my father won't consider the path of peace. I have to do something."

Talor's gaze narrowed. "And what will freeing me achieve?"

Annoyance flashed across her features. "Do you want to live or not, Eagle?"

"Denying me my right to vengeance seems a high price to pay," Talor replied, his voice lowering to a growl.

"So, you'd rather die ... freeze to death like a dog out here in the snow?"

Heat kindled in Talor's belly. Anger wreathed up inside him like smoke. He welcomed the sensation, as it distracted him from the gnawing, biting cold.

When he did not answer, Mor drew closer still. Tension bracketed her mouth, and Talor suddenly realized that she was nervous. "I've sent the guards away," she said tightly. "The next shift will arrive soon ... you won't have another chance to escape. What is your answer?"

Their gazes fused for a heartbeat. Her closeness enveloped Talor; he could feel the heat of her body radiating out toward him. How he wished he too was wrapped in furs. The moment was charged, and despite that anger now pulsed like a stoked ember within him, Talor knew he was being offered his last chance at survival.

He might have been hotheaded and insanely rash, but he wasn't a complete fool. He still did not understand how this woman thought she was going to benefit from freeing him, but he was not going to stop her.

"Very well," he ground out the words. "I swear that I will not seek revenge again on your father." He paused then, the moment drawing out between them. "Can you cut me down now?"

Talor collapsed on to his knees the moment Mor released the shackles from around his wrists. Muttering a curse under his breath, he tried to rise to his feet and failed. "This isn't going to work," he wheezed. "I can't walk."

"You're going to have to," Mor growled back, her voice flint-hard. "I can't drag you."

The harshness of her voice, her utter lack of sympathy for his situation, galvanized Talor. He was not going to let this Serpent woman dominate him. "Help me up then," he snarled back. "It's both our necks on the line now."

A moment later her hand fastened around his arm, and together they managed to get him to his feet. Then, Mor shoved a shoulder under Talor's armpit, bearing much of his weight. Together they stumbled forward, through the deepening snow.

The blizzard had not lessened all afternoon, and as the last of the daylight faded from the world, Talor realized with a sinking sensation that it was probably going to snow all night as well.

The white-out was a mixed blessing. With the snow falling so thickly no one would be able to follow them, for their tracks would be covered almost immediately. The downside was that they would be traveling blindly in such weather.

But this was his only chance to escape, and he would take it.

Mor led him around the base of the broch, across the empty yard before the front steps, and under the archway that led out into the village. Talor lurched forward, gritting his teeth as he forced each foot in front of the other. He had never found walking so hard. His body would not cooperate with him. Yet with each step, he found the blood returning to his limbs, rushing through his numb legs and arms. Unfortunately, the sensation brought pain with it, and Talor had to bite down on his tongue to stop a groan escaping.

Craning his neck up as they passed through the archway, Talor spied the outline of two guards atop the wall a few yards distant. However, they were facing away from them—and Mor and Talor passed into the village unnoticed.

The weather was so foul that there did not appear to be anyone about. To Talor's surprise, Mor seemed to know her way about the fort as well as he did. She moved confidently, her path never wavering. He realized then that she was taking him to the south gate, a narrow gateway that led down a steep path to the stony beach south of the fort.

Although the gate was closed, they found no warriors guarding it.

"Where is everyone?" Talor asked through gritted teeth. His hands and feet were throbbing dully now.

Torches hung on the wall next to a burning brazier. Mor helped herself to one, and lit it, before casting Talor a sidelong glance. "I sent the guards away," she replied, her tone clipped. "I told them that, owing to the blizzard, they could end their shift early tonight and that others would arrive shortly to replace them. On a night like this, those on the watch are relieved to be able to get indoors. None of the warriors questioned me."

Talor was not surprised by this news—Mor was the chieftain's daughter after all.

Leaving Talor standing on his own, Mor moved forward and unbarred the gate. She then used her shoulder to open it wide enough for them to get through.

"I wanted to get us ponies," she said, beckoning to him to follow her. "But I think that would have been stretching our good fortune."

Talor could see her point. Sneaking out on foot was one thing—stealing two ponies without being spotted was another. Nonetheless, he could have done with a pony to carry him.

He shuffled forward, grateful that his limbs were now cooperating with him at least, and followed Mor out of the gate.

He then hauled it shut behind him and turned to face his unlikely savior.

Mor's face, illuminated by the torch she held aloft, was set in hard, determined lines. "Here." She shrugged off her fur mantle, and Talor saw that she wore another cloak underneath. She handed him the fur. "I brought this for you."

Giving a grunt of thanks, Talor cast the mantle over his shoulders. Almost instantly he started to feel better. His hands and feet ached, and his teeth chattered, but the heavy cloak provided a barrier from the seeking wind and bone numbing chill.

Maybe the Gods were with him after all—it did not look as if he was going to freeze tonight. Not yet anyway.

Chapter Nine

Lead the Way

SHORTLY AFTER LEAVING Dun Ringill, Mor realized that she had no idea where she was taking them.

Halting, she turned to Talor. "I think I'm getting us lost," she admitted. "You'd better take the lead."

His face, illuminated by the glow of her torch, looked strained and pale. He had been close to succumbing to the cold when she approached him earlier. She had almost left it too late.

She had almost not come at all.

She could not believe she had embarked on this folly. Knots twisted in her belly as she thought of her father's reaction when he discovered both his daughter and his prisoner gone. He would be so hurt by her act. She knew he would never recover from it—but she had to do this.

Yet it would only be worthwhile if they did not wander around in circles all night.

Fortunately for them both, the snow had eased a little, as had the wind. The torch she carried had nearly guttered and died a number of times in the first stretch of the journey. Yet it burned brightly now, illuminating the snow-covered hillside they trudged up.

But despite that the visibility was better than it had been, Mor had completely lost any sense of direction.

With a sigh, Talor took the torch from her. "We are south-east of the fort now," he replied. His voice was rough, edged in pain. He was tough; she would give him that. Mor had been hard on him when he had struggled to rise after being chained to the wall for so long. But the reality was that she was surprised how well he had coped.

The folk of this isle were resilient indeed.

"I suggest we turn east and head directly inland," Talor continued. "There is a stag hunters' hut in one of the valleys. We can shelter there."

Mor's tension eased slightly at these words. A hut. Somewhere they could take refuge from the cold and possibly even light a fire. "How far away is it?" she asked.

Talor held her gaze. His blue eyes were not friendly. There was a reserve in him, a hostility that bubbled just beneath the surface. He had agreed not to kill her father, but they were far from friends.

Even so, there was something about this man that made it hard for her to look away. That fascination surfaced once more, and she found her gaze devouring him. She wanted to know what Talor mac Donnel was thinking.

"It will probably take us most of the night to reach the hut," he replied finally.

Mor's burgeoning hope splintered at this news. A roof over her head and a warm fire would have to wait a while.

"Very well," she huffed. She then pulled up the hood of her cloak, doing her best to protect her face from the stinging cold. "Lead the way."

It felt like the longest journey of Mor's life.

She slogged through the snow, just a couple of feet behind Talor. He carried the torch now, and although it had stopped snowing for the time being, she was amazed that Talor walked so confidently. Some of the snowdrifts were knee deep in places.

And as they traveled, Mor tried not to dwell on what she had done, what she had left behind. She had no plan, only a dogged determination to somehow weave peace. Every time her thoughts settled upon this fact, anxiety fluttered up within her like a trapped bird.

This has to be done, she reminded herself grimly, shoving down her panic. *If there had been another way, I would have taken it.*

A sea of undulating hills stretched east, and then gradually, the land became rougher, the dips between the rise of each hill deeper. It slowed their progress, and when they passed a copse of birch trees, Talor broke off a branch and used it to feel out the land before him.

"The land is uneven here," he explained, as he continued his way forward. "You could easily walk into a hole and end up with a broken leg." Mor heard the rasp of exhaustion in his voice. Her own body was starting to protest as the night wore on, and she could only imagine how he felt. The man had suffered serious beatings. Not only that, but he had barely eaten since being taken prisoner. If they did not reach their destination soon, he would collapse.

They continued on, and it was not long before Talor started to stagger. Drawing up alongside him, Mor cut her companion a look. "We should rest," she announced. "If you continue, you're going to fall over."

Talor glowered at her. "I'm well."

"You're staggering as if you just consumed a barrel of mead," she pointed out dryly. "We both know you're far from well, so stop pretending otherwise."

Talor halted, leaning on his stick for support. He shut his eyes briefly, and when they opened, she saw desperation flicker in their depths. They both knew the truth of it. He was reaching the end of his endurance.

"The hut isn't far," he said, his voice rough. "If my memory serves me correctly, we should find it at the end of this valley."

Mor nodded, relief rising within her. "Come on then."

She stepped close to him and, reaching out, took the guttering torch. Very soon it would sputter and die. Without it they would be traveling blind. A starry sky had appeared briefly earlier, but now a bank of clouds had passed before it, and the snow was starting to flutter down once more. They really needed to get to that hut.

"Lean on my shoulder," Mor instructed.

Talor shook his head, stubbornness lighting in his eyes.

"Do it, Eagle." Mor did not have any patience for his stubbornness. "I don't want to have to drag you the rest of the way."

With a muttered curse, Talor did as instructed, allowing Mor to slide her shoulder under his elbow so that he could wrap one arm around her shoulders. His weight dragged her down, reminding Mor that fatigue pressed down upon her as well. Her toes now throbbed with cold, even through her boots, and she could feel the chill biting through her layers of clothing. Nevertheless, she knew that she could have traveled for a while longer. Talor could not.

They staggered on together, entwined like lovers, as they made their way down a narrow vale. Boulders surrounded them, peeking up through the snow. And just as the torch was on the verge of dying, Mor spied a squat shape ahead.

Her breathing caught, and relief hit her. The hut. They had reached it at last.

Made of stacked stone, with a conical roof covered with sods, the hut was tiny—barely big enough for a hunting party of four warriors to sit comfortably within. Relief slammed into Mor as they struggled down the valley. The hut represented survival.

Stooping, she entered the dwelling, hauling Talor in after her.

Breathing another curse, he sank to the ground. The door to the hut had been left open, and as such, snow had fluttered in. Yet most of the space was dry. An unlit hearth sat in the center of the dwelling. The last hunters to stay here had kindly left a fresh lump of peat in the fire pit. It was a hunter's tradition that when you left a hut, you did your best to make the next visitors welcome. Without that lump of peat, it would have been impossible to light a fire, for she could not go foraging for firewood.

Mor unslung the leather pack she had donned underneath her cloak. It had been difficult to help herself to the supplies she needed before leaving, but she had managed to pack her flint, tinder, a bladder of water, and a parcel of curd-cheese dumplings leftover from that night's supper. The dumplings had actually been meant for the guards keeping watch on the wall. It had been a good excuse, both to leave the broch, and to don her cloak and take the food without arousing suspicion. It had been a risk, but seeing the gaunt lines on Talor's face, Mor was relieved she had made the effort to bring food.

He needed to eat.

Once again, her concern for this man's welfare surprised Mor.

She was a warrior, born and raised to be ruthless. A female warrior had to be even more cold-blooded at times than her male counterparts. It was a natural female tendency to nurture, to take care of others' needs. Such an instinct could get you killed in battle. Mor had learned to quash it from an early age.

But this man, this enemy, brought out a side in her she did not know she possessed. It was odd, for his arrogance was abrasive.

You need to keep him alive, she counselled herself. Desperation wreathed up within Mor like wood smoke. She hated not having a plan. *You can't weave peace alone.*

That was it, she assured herself. She did not actually care what happened to this warrior. But what she did care about was ensuring that the rest of her people, who now sheltered at Dun Ringill, survived. She had to save them.

The first thing Mor did was get the fire lit. Her flint and tinder did the work, and shortly after the peat was alight. It was slightly damp and hissed as it burned, omitting a thick, pungent smoke that tickled the back of Mor's throat. Nevertheless, the heat was welcome.

Talor had drawn close to the fire pit and was lying on his side now. The fur mantle she had given him draped over his torso and legs, although his face was worryingly pale.

Mor unwrapped the food she had brought and handed him a dumpling. "Here," she murmured. "You need to eat."

He took the dumpling with a nod before devouring it. She then handed him another before passing him the bladder of water as well.

"Thank you," Talor finally grunted.

Mor fought the urge to smile. She knew it had cost him to thank his enemy.

Sitting back, Mor poked at the burning peat with a stick, rousing it. "This fire doesn't feel like it's putting out enough heat," she grumbled.

"It does to me," Talor replied. He had eaten and drunk, and a little color had returned to his cheeks.

Silence fell between them then. Now that they had fled Dun Ringill, and completed their journey safely to the mountains, there was nothing to do but wait the rest of the night out. Still, Mor could tell from Talor's shuttered expression that he was wary of her. The bruises and swelling on his face added a harshness to his look. He still did not trust her, despite that she had saved his life.

He was watching her under half-lowered lids, and when he spoke once more, there was a suspicious edge to his voice. "What now, Serpent?"

"Now, we rest and regain our strength."

"You do realize you can't go back?"

Mor clenched her jaw. She really did not need reminding. "I'm aware of that."

"And how exactly do you think this is going to weave peace? The Serpent have no right to our lands."

"I'm not sure yet," she admitted her tone sharpening. "I didn't have time to come up with a detailed plan ... you were freezing to death, remember?"

Talor snorted. "You've betrayed your people for nothing."

Mor went still, even as anger stirred in her belly. She leaned forward, her gaze seizing Talor's. "It's not for nothing," she growled. "I intend to make this count."

Chapter Ten

A Crossroads

BLINKING, TALOR straightened up outside the hut. Compared to the dim interior, the morning was blinding in its brightness. A hard blue sky and glittering sun reflected off a white world. Talor reached up and shaded his eyes as they teared from the intensity.

He had not thought he would live to see another sunrise.

It still amazed him that he had.

Still shading his eyes from the reflected whiteness, Talor trudged away from the hut, circling behind it to where a boulder jutted out of the snow. There, he unlaced his breaches and relieved his bladder. Releasing a sigh, Talor closed his eyes and tilted his face up to the sun. It was a balm upon his bruised, swollen, and aching face. Fortunately, the injuries he had sustained from the beatings were more superficial than he had originally thought. There did not appear to be any fractured or broken bones. His body was covered in bruises and grazes, but he usually healed quickly, and they would fade in days.

Talor opened his eyes and took stock of what his situation now was. He had woken up in a daze inside. For a moment, as he stirred under the heavy fur mantle, he had imagined he was back in Balintur sleeping by the fire in his own hut. But then he had opened his eyes and spied the woman with flame-red hair sleeping opposite him—and everything flooded back.

Talor rubbed a hand over his face and muttered a curse. He could not believe he had sworn to that woman that he would not seek further vengeance upon her father. Now that he was far from Dun Ringill, and alive, the need for revenge kindled once more in the pit of his belly.

He could not let it go.

She had given him little choice. It was either agree or die. And, if he was honest, even when she freed him from his chains, he had been skeptical that they would manage to flee safely.

But here they were.

Talor trudged back to the entrance of the hut. Before going inside, he paused, his keen gaze sweeping the valley. Snow covered everything, including the stand of firs that carpeted the steep eastern side of the valley. The wintry scene made the landscape look so different. In the summer, a stream trickled through the heart of the vale, but snow completely covered the waterway now. It was probably frozen solid. He was pleased to see though that the white crust around them was completely pristine; there were no signs of their footprints leading to the hut, which meant that the snow had continued to fall during the night and would have obscured their tracks leading here. The Serpent chieftain would not be able to follow them.

A harsh smile tugged at Talor's lips. He thought just how angry Cathal mac Calum would be right now. It brightened his mood just a little.

Ducking back into the hut, Talor found Mor awake. She was seated cross-legged, rousing the glowing embers of the fire with a stick. She had added another lump of peat to it, and although the air was close and smoky inside the hut, it was welcomingly warm.

Lowering himself down onto his fur cloak, Talor also adopted a cross-legged position, wincing as he did so.

"How are the bruises?" Mor asked, handing him a cold dumpling.

Talor took the food, his mouth filling with saliva. He was absolutely starving this morning. "They hurt," he replied. "But they'll heal soon enough."

"I'm surprised you aren't more seriously injured," Mor replied. "Tormud must have gone softly on you."

Talor's mouth twisted. "He was probably hoping to get me on his own later."

Mor's full mouth curved. It was a very slight smile, but it transformed her face. Seated before the hearth, her fiery hair tumbling down over her shoulders, the glow of the flames bathing her milky skin, she was the most striking woman he had ever set eyes on. She had wrapped her fur cloak around her shoulders for warmth, but he could see her long, shapely legs, clad in close-fitting plaid breeches, folded underneath it.

Not for the first time since their initial meeting, he felt heat build in his loins at the mere sight of her.

Talor clenched his jaw. His body's reaction angered him, and he attempted to ignore his attraction to this woman. He was sick of having these animalistic urges every time he locked eyes with Mor. He could never lose sight of the fact that she was his enemy—he had to be wary of her.

But Mor had also saved his life, and that complicated matters.

Talor swallowed the last mouthful of dumpling. He could have eaten many more of them, but saw that they now only had two left. This time of year, there were very few animals and birds to hunt out here in the wilderness. That was the last of their food. Mor was wisely rationing the supplies.

"We slept late," Mor said after a pause. Her voice was reserved, her gaze shuttered. "It's nearly noon."

Watching her, Talor had the sense that this was a woman who was used to keeping her emotions locked down. She gave very little away. Having grown up with a sensitive, emotional step-mother, Talor found Mor's coldness strange.

"I'm not surprised," Talor replied, his own tone guarded. "We spent most of the night traveling to get here." He paused, his gaze narrowing. "Do any of your people know about this hut?"

Mor shook her head. "None, I'd guess. The only one you have to worry about is Tormud ... but he doesn't come from this part of the isle, and he's been away for the past two decades."

"They shouldn't be able to follow us here," Talor informed her. "The snow has covered our tracks."

Relief flickered in those beautiful moss green eyes. He had rarely seen eyes that color; it suited her pale, freckled skin and auburn hair.

Stop it. He gave himself a mental shake. The last thing he wanted to do was sit here admiring the color of this woman's eyes. *She is the enemy. Never forget that.*

Another silence drew out, and this time Talor broke it. "Why did you free me?" he asked, aware of the aggressive edge to his voice. She needed to know that he did not trust her, not one bit.

Mor exhaled slowly, as if his question wearied her. "I told you, back at Dun Ringill. I've had enough of war, of feuding, I had to break the cycle."

Talor's brow furrowed. He was not exactly sure what she meant. But he thought she was being a fool. "Freeing me isn't going to achieve much."

She shook her head. "No ... but it's the first step."

Talor drew back slightly, his frown deepening. "Toward what?"

She held his gaze, hers unnervingly steady. "To peace, Talor." The way she said his name caused heat to arrow through his groin. "Between your people and mine. I want The Serpent to remain upon The Winged Isle ... for us to put down roots here."

Their gazes fused for a long heartbeat. And then Talor threw back his head and barked a laugh. "There will be no peace between our people. Not now, not ever. You've gone too far for that. You've shed too much blood."

That got a reaction from her. He watched as Mor's features tightened, as a faint flush crept across her high cheekbones, and those moss-colored eyes darkened to a deep pine green. "You're wrong," she replied, an edge of panic to her voice. "It's not too late. If we work together, we can stop this. Maybe you and I can find a way to make both sides see sense."

Talor drew in a sharp breath. If she had slapped him across the face, he would have been less shocked. "I'm not working with you."

Her gaze narrowed. "Why not?"

Talor leaned forward, his gaze never leaving hers. Anger pulsed through him, although he could see that he had succeeded in infuriating her as well. The Mother preserve him, she was even more striking when riled. He could see a magnificent bosom heaving beneath her mantle.

"You arrived on our shores, uninvited," he began, his voice roughening. "You pillaged our villages, killed my family and friends ... there is no way we will make peace with you. The ocean will boil, and the moon will crash to the earth, before that ever happens."

"You're being pigheaded," she growled out the words now. "I too have lost those I love to this conflict." He saw her gaze gutter as she admitted this. "But the fact remains that there is still time to make peace."

Talor craned his neck forward, as rage now ignited within him. It pounded through his veins, hot and reckless. He itched to strike out, to hurt those who had harmed the ones he loved. Those who had brought so much grief to his people. "I hope this campaign has cost you dearly," he said, his voice low and hard. "I hope it has stripped away everything from you."

Her gaze guttered further, and misgiving twisted Talor's gut, before he shoved it aside. *No pity for these people. Ever.*

"I lost both my brothers," she replied, her voice low and flat. "They meant as much to me as your sister did to you. I could take my vengeance upon you for their deaths, but I choose not to."

"Well that's not my choice," Talor spat out the words. "I choose to finish this the way it started. With blood."

"What are you going to do?" There was a taunting edge to her voice, and a nerve flickered in her cheek, hinting at the emotions churning beneath her controlled exterior. She was truly angry now. He only had to push her just a little bit further, and he would get what he wanted: a fight. "We stripped you of all your weapons, Eagle. Are you going to try and kill me with your bare hands?"

"What I'm going to do is leave this hut, and you, behind," he snarled. "I'm going to march back to Dun Ringill, and I'm going to rip your father's heart out."

"Treacherous dog, you swore an oath!"

"Under duress. You can't strip a warrior of his need for vengeance. Your father's had it coming ... you've all had it coming."

And with that, Talor rose to his feet and made for the door.

He never reached it, for Mor barreled into him. Talor flew backward and crashed onto the floor. Pain exploded through his body, as the injuries that had not even yet started to heal properly protested at such rough treatment. "Bastard." A fist slammed into his jaw. "You dare go back on your oath, and I'll kill you."

Talor hit back, anger giving him a strength he did not even realize he possessed. Despite that he was bruised, cold, and exhausted—he had regained some strength after having eaten and rested. Rage did the rest.

Their fists flew as they rolled over and over on the dirt floor of the hut, cursing and snarling at each other.

Talor landed a few solid punches, one to her belly and another to her jaw, but Mor punched back just as hard. Agony exploded in Talor's skull as her knuckles slammed into his bruised ribs; unlike her, his body could not withstand much more of a beating.

But that did not stop him from fighting. Wrath flowed out of him in a molten tide. Talor forgot his aches and pains, forgot everything except his loathing for these people. They had torn his life down. They had destroyed his world.

This woman had saved him, and he should have been grateful to her. But if she had been wise, she would have left him to die in the cold.

They were mortal enemies. They would never be anything else.

Mor's knee drove into his gut, while he grabbed a handful of her hair and tried to smash her head down against the floor. With a curse, she head-butted him. The world darkened, and for a moment Talor thought he would lose consciousness. His vision blurred, and he slackened his hold on her.

Snarling another curse, Mor pushed herself off him.

As Talor came to, shaking his head to clear it, his gaze settled upon her. She was crouched a few feet away, poised to spring at him again should he give her a reason.

"You can die right here," she panted. "If that's what you really want?" Mor spat on the ground between them then, making her disdain for him clear. "I saved you because I thought you too might want an end to this bloodshed." Her lip curled then. "But it appears I misjudged you. I took you to be a better man than you actually are."

Her insults washed off Talor. All the same, he did not make a move to attack her. Instead, clenching his jaw as his bruised belly tormented him, he rolled onto his side. "That was your mistake then," he growled. "You're clearly a poor judge of character."

"Enough," she countered. "I tire of listening to your venom. If you won't help me, then you're of no use to me." In one smooth movement, she unsheathed the blade she had strapped to her thigh. "Maybe I'll just cut your throat and be done with it."

Talor stared at her. He had grown up amongst warrior women. His aunt Tea was fierce, and his cousin

Fina was a warrior to be reckoned with despite that most men towered over her. But this woman was something else. There was a core of iron inside her, and the rage on her face only made her beauty burn brighter.

The Hag shrivel his cods, Mor was something to behold.

If anyone was going to slit his throat, he would prefer it was her.

And yet, at that moment, the survival instinct surged once more, cutting through the madness of his rage. Once again it occurred to him that he really did not want to die. He stared back at Mor, watching the firelight glint off her blade, and realized that he had truly reached a crossroads.

Death or compromise. He had a choice to make.

Chapter Eleven

Keeping Oaths

THE CRACKLE OF the hearth and their ragged breathing were the only sounds inside the hut. Eventually, Talor broke the tense standoff between them. "I'd rather you didn't slit my throat, woman."

"Then you need to cooperate with me," she replied, her voice flint hard. "Enough of the insults, enough of the hate. I'm done with it."

Talor grimaced and rubbed his aching forehead. He regarded her warily. "That's hardly a strategy," he replied. "Last time I asked, you didn't have a plan ... has that changed?" He knew his comment was arrogant, and he had injected a challenge into his voice deliberately.

Mor's dark auburn brows knitted together for a moment, before she slowly lowered her blade, re-sheathing it. She moved away from him then, returning to her side of the fire. But her gaze never left him. She was still wary of him, and was right to be.

"We need guidance," she said finally. "If we are to change the course of things between our peoples, someone must help us."

Talor folded his arms across his chest. "Who exactly?"

Her mouth thinned. He was still deliberately goading her, and he could see her temper still simmered. Talor knew he was being an unreasonable, rude bastard, but he just could not seem to stop himself. The urge to lash out was too strong.

"We should go and see Old Murdina," Mor said finally. "She's the bandruí of my tribe."

Talor stiffened. "We can't go back to Dun Ringill." He pointed out. "We'll get caught."

Mor shook her head. "Our seer doesn't live within the walls of the fort," she replied. "She dwells in a cave on the shore south of Dun Ringill. Do you know it?"

Talor nodded. Of course he knew the cave. He had played in it often enough as a child, and had first lain with a woman there. His lover was a lass he had spent a summer with, years earlier. As the warm weather waned, so did his interest, and although she had been upset, the girl soon found solace in the arms of another. She was wed now and had recently given birth to her second child. There were no hard feelings between them these days.

"It's still too close to the fort," he said after a pause. "It'll be risky to approach it."

"That's why we should wait until dusk," she replied. Mor leaned back, a little of the tension ebbing from her shoulders. "If we leave here during the afternoon, we will reach the cave as night falls. It should be easier to arrive unseen."

Talor watched her a moment. He did not like this idea. He had a lot of respect for his cousin Ailene, their own tribe's bandruí, but he did not know Old Murdina. Some seers were said to be full of malice and cunning. You could not trust them all. The woman might try to manipulate them, or she might betray them to Cathal.

"Won't the bandruí just go straight to your father?" he asked after a pause.

Mor huffed a bitter laugh, before she ran a hand over her face. The act revealed the strain she was under. She hid it well, but betraying her own people was costing her. "Old Murdina won't say a word to my father," she replied softly. "She can't stand him."

They set out from the hut, bathed in wintry sunshine. At first it looked as if the good weather was going to linger and the snow might just start to melt. But as they trekked west, out of the heart of the mountains and across the rolling hills that stretched toward the coast, the sky darkened. The pinkish hue on the horizon warned that the good weather had merely been a respite. More snow was coming.

Even so, the break in the weather made traveling easier.

Mor allowed Talor to lead the way. She did not take her eyes off him as he walked. Her gaze bored a hole in his back.

No one had ever incensed her like he had back in the hut. For a few rage-fueled moments, she had wanted to kill him.

Her belly still ached from the blow he had delivered, and her left cheekbone felt swollen and tender to the touch where his knuckles had grazed it. Nevertheless, she had delivered a few damaging blows of her own, and she had not lied to him: she had been ready to slit his throat with her knife in the end. He had pushed her to the limit, and she had sorely regretted saving his hide.

He did not deserve it.

Nonetheless, in the end he listened to her. She had seen the suspicion in his gaze. He did not like the idea of going to the seer. But then he was not keen to ally himself with her at all.

Talor was short on options at this point. Old Murdina would also have food, and they could take shelter in her cave overnight before deciding on their next move.

Mor continued to watch Talor as they traveled west, her gaze taking in the breadth of his shoulders, accentuated by the fur cloak he wore. Unlike most

Cruthini men, he had cut his dark hair short. It was a severe style that gave an edge to his good looks. And even though he bore numerous injuries, and was struggling through deep snow, she noticed the lithe, fluid way in which he moved. It was a predatory stride. And despite everything, the heat of attraction resurfaced once more, pooling in her core.

He was the rudest, most aggravating man she had ever met, and yet her attraction to him had not diminished. On the contrary, it had grown.

By mid-afternoon, the sky had completely clouded over and a sharp wind gusted in from the north. Shortly after that, the snow started to flutter down once more. Fortunately, they were half way toward their destination now, and Talor seemed to know exactly where he was headed. Of course, he had grown up in these lands, had hunted and patrolled these hills since he was a lad. He did not hesitate as he traveled west.

The days were short this time of year, and so dusk came upon them all too soon. A murky, snowy gloaming made visibility difficult. But still, Talor did not slow his pace. Mor hurried after him, hoping that he really was as confident as he appeared.

And then, as the last of the light faded, they reached the coast.

Through the swirling snow, Mor spied the fires of Dun Ringill. The fort perched like a beacon upon the clifftop a few furlongs away. The braziers atop its walls cast a golden light that could be seen in every direction for quite some distance. Spying it as well, Talor drew to a halt. The action was so sudden that Mor nearly ran into the back of him. She stepped up next to her companion and shifted her gaze to his profile, noting the hawkish set of his features.

She did not like the expression she saw there.

"You promised," she said, her voice low and hard. "Doesn't an oath mean anything to you?"

Talor turned to her then, his gaze seizing hers. For a moment she thought he might argue with her again, that he might deliberately provoke her like he had in the hut.

But a shadow passed over his features instead, still visible despite that the light had almost faded completely. "Lucky for you, an Eagle warrior keeps his word," Talor replied.

Watching him, it dawned on Mor that his behavior back in the hut had been aimed at goading her. She suspected he had never intended to break his oath—what he had wanted was a fight.

Before she could question Talor about it, he turned from her, leading the way down the steep, snowy bank. "Follow me ... the cave is just up ahead."

"Murdina," Mor called out softly as she treaded through the snowdrift at the mouth of the cave. "Are you there?"

For a moment dread twisted her stomach, as she feared the seer might have left the cave and taken refuge at the fort, driven out of her cold, damp home by the snow. But then she spied the glow of a fire up ahead, and her belly relaxed.

The bandruí was here after all.

"Come forward," a cool, whispery voice called out. "Who is it who disturbs me on such a night?"

"It's me ... Mor."

A pause followed, and when the voice spoke again, it was a lot warmer. "Come forward, lass."

Mor stepped through into the cave itself. A messy space greeted her. Murdina had only dwelt here a few months, and already it looked as if this cave had been her home for years.

Piles of animal bones and stacks of drying herbs lay upon the floor, and a heap of peat sods had been stored up against one wall. As she entered, Mor's gaze slid past a row of wooden cages. Each one housed a different creature. She glimpsed a stoat, a gull, a goose, and a black rat. The rat peered up at her with gleaming eyes.

Mor's attention did not remain upon the cages for long—instead, it shifted to the tiny woman seated before the fire.

She had known Old Murdina her whole life, and even when she had been a bairn, the bandruí had always seemed ancient to her. A network of deep lines carved her round face, although her sunken smoke-grey eyes were cunning. As always, the seer was garbed in a long sleeveless tunic, her frail body weighed down by an assortment of jewelry made from bone. Around her thin shoulders she wore a fur cloak to ward off the chill, and heavy fur boots covered her feet. During the warmer months, Murdina went barefoot.

"I heard that you had gone missing," Old Murdina greeted Mor, her gaze as sharp as ever. The bandruí's attention shifted then to the man entering the cave behind her. "And that you'd freed your father's prisoner."

Mor glanced over her shoulder at Talor, judging his reaction. Unsurprisingly, he was frowning; his lean, muscular frame tense as he watched the seer.

"Talor mac Donnel," Old Murdina murmured, raising a gnarled hand to beckon him closer. "I have heard all about your brave yet reckless deed. Cathal must be going soft with age if you still breathe."

Talor did not answer. Instead, he moved forward, stepping up next to Mor in the circle of the firelight.

Observing him, a smile stretched across the crone's face. Then, to Mor's consternation, the seer licked her lips. "Ah, it all becomes clear now," she said, her voice developing a crooning edge. "No wonder you saved this one's life, Mor. He's a feast for the eyes."

Chapter Twelve

What Must Be Done

THE BANDRUÍ'S WORDS made Mor's cheeks warm. She had not brought Talor here so that Old Murdina could make lecherous comments. Casting a look at Talor's profile, she saw that his expression had not changed. His blue eyes were shuttered as he continued to watch the seer.

Old Murdina rose to her feet, her bone jewelry rattling. Drawing her fur close around her shoulders, she shuffled over to Talor. Watching her, Mor wondered just how old Murdina was. She was kin to Mor, for she had been her mother's great aunt. Lena had been very close to the seer, had followed her advice on all things. Mor knew that her father resented the closeness of their relationship—been jealous of it even. Ever since Lena's death, he only sought Old Murdina's advice when circumstance forced it.

The seer drew close to Talor and craned her neck, gazing up at him.

Wordlessly, she then reached up a hand, her wizened fingers tracing the lines of his face. "Even beaten and bruised you are quite a sight," Old Murdina murmured.

Mor noted that Talor did not react to her touch. He did not flinch away as her father might have, nor did he appear to stiffen. Instead, he merely watched her, his face inscrutable now.

Old Murdina's smile turned wolfish as she trailed one hand down his neck, and splayed her palm over his heart. "If I was forty years younger, I'd invite you to my furs," she said, before giving a soft cackle.

Mor's embarrassment flamed hotter. "Murdina," she said, her voice sharp. "Talor isn't here to be—"

"Quiet, lass," the crone cut her off. "I'll get to you in a moment ... but first your friend here has my full attention."

Watching Talor, Mor saw the way his body stiffened at the word 'friend'. However, he still did not move away from the bandruí's bold touch. His mouth curved just a little as he held the old woman's gaze, as if her words amused him.

Mor clenched her jaw. Surely he was not going to encourage Old Murdina?

"You are an interesting one, Talor mac Donnel," the seer said after a pause. "Your history is steeped in blood and sorrow ... and yet there is strength in you ... and great courage." Old Murdina inclined her head then, as if being in physical contact with the warrior told her things. "You never knew your mother ... she died either in birthing you or soon after."

Talor's faint smile faded, yet he still did not speak.

After a moment the bandruí continued. "Your father ... he is quite a man too ... a great warrior, feared by many."

"Next you're going to tell me that I lost my half-sister in battle recently ... that it was Cathal himself who slew her." Talor did speak then. His voice was low, dangerous.

Old Murdina cackled at this, removing her hand from his chest but not stepping back from him. "I already know all that, lad. Cathal himself was here earlier today.

He told me who you were, and why you'd tried to kill him. But you never told him of your family history, did you?"

A nerve flickered in Talor's cheek. "And what else do you know of me?"

The bandruí favored him with another sly smile. "I know that you attract women to you easily as breathing … and yet you have never been in love."

Talor did react then; a faint blush stained his cheekbones, and he took a step back from Murdina, his eyebrows raising. "A lucky guess, I'd say, old woman."

The seer gave another wheezing laugh. "Of course."

Old Murdina shifted her attention to Mor then, her gaze raking over her from head to foot. "And as for you … this was something I also foresaw."

Mor stepped closer to the bandruí, frowning. "What do you mean?"

"Your father came to me a few months ago, looking for advice."

"Aye, and you told him that blood would be spilled before Mid-Winter Fire."

Old Murdina's mouth twisted. "That's not all I told him." The crone fingered one of the many bone bracelets that encircled her thin wrists, before she continued. "I also advised him that one of those in his inner circle would betray him … and you just have."

Heat flushed through Mor. "I haven't."

The seer raised a silvery eyebrow. "And what do you call freeing a prisoner and escaping from the fort with him? You should have witnessed your father today … I've never seen him so angry."

The gleam in Old Murdina's eyes revealed that she had enjoyed seeing Cathal in such a state. The dislike went both ways, it seemed.

"This … wasn't a betrayal," Mor choked out the words once more. "I didn't do this to hurt my father, but to help him."

"And how is that?"

"You've seen what he's like, Murdina. Since Ma died, he has focused on glory for our people and nothing else.

When he lost my brothers, he became even more blinkered. Artair has tried to talk to him about leaving the isle. I want him to negotiate peace so we can stay here, yet he won't hear a word of it ... something had to be done."

Mor broke off there, aware that Talor's gaze was upon her. A frown marred his brow as he studied her, his gaze wary.

The bandruí also watched her, a thoughtful expression upon her face. "You hope to weave peace by freeing your father's prisoner?"

"Aye, but I have no idea what to do next. We need your help, Murdina. Please guide us ... tell us what must be done in order to end this conflict."

A shadow moved in the old woman's pale grey eyes. Her face went unusually grave then. "Bloodshed is a way of life for our people, lass. It has been for generations now."

Mor held the seer's gaze, her own never wavering. "Then perhaps it's time to take a new path."

"You'd go against your own father to achieve this?"

Mor swallowed hard. "If that's what it takes." They were brave words, although each one of them stabbed her in the heart. She adored her father, hated the thought of him being angry or disappointed with her. But the time to worry about pleasing Cathal was over. She had spent too many years following him unquestioningly. This campaign was wrong. She had to help end it.

"I will do a reading," the seer said.

More inhaled sharply. "Thank you."

Old Murdina's face twisted. "Don't thank me yet, lass ... you might not like what I tell you."

With that, the seer cast Talor a shrewd look. "Can you fetch me the stoat from one of those cages?"

Talor's mouth compressed at the request. Then, after a heavy pause, he nodded. Without a word, he moved past Mor to the cages at the back of the cave. The animals and birds within shifted nervously, as if sensing his intent. Talor approached the cage at one end containing the stoat. The creature shrank back, teeth baring, and Talor hesitated.

"Go on, lad," Old Murdina urged, a note of glee in her voice. "I wouldn't mess around if I were you. Stoats have sharp teeth."

Mor cast the bandruí an irritated look. She was enjoying herself a bit too much.

Talor's expression darkened, before he opened the top of the cage and thrust his hand inside, pulling out the small, wriggling creature. The stoat was pretty, with a chestnut body, a white belly, and a black-tipped tail. Talor had sensibly gripped it around the neck, yet it clawed and snarled at him all the same as he turned and carried it over to where Old Murdina waited.

The seer met Talor on the other side of the fire. She grabbed the stoat and wrung its neck in one swift movement, before flinging its corpse onto the dusty ground. Then, drawing a thin blade from her belt, the seer knelt and slit open the hapless rodent's belly.

Mor's bile rose as a foul smell permeated the air of the cave. Old Murdina did not appear to even notice or care. Instead, she pulled out the stoat's entrails, laying them upon the dusty floor. Then, she held them up to the firelight, studying the offal intently. Picking up the liver first, and then the long rope of the intestines.

The seer's face screwed up as she peered at the entrails, a study in concentration.

Neither Talor nor Mor interrupted her.

Eventually, Old Murdina lowered the grisly objects and sat back on her heels. Her gaze swept from Mor to Talor. Mor frowned as she stared back at the crone; the seer wore a sly smile upon her face.

"I have advice for you," the bandruí said finally, "although neither of you is going to like it."

"Out with it then," Talor said, his voice sharp now. Was Mor imagining it, or had he grown uneasy. Tension rippled off him as he regarded the seer with a cool stare.

The bandruí climbed to her feet, wincing as her old bones protested. "There is a way forward ... a way to ensure that our people all survive the coming year." Her gaze flicked between the two of them once more, before she continued. "If you want to bring peace to this isle, then you two must wed."

Silence followed this proclamation.

Suddenly, all Mor could hear was the roar of her own breathing. It was so loud that it obliterated the crackle and pop of the hearth, the whistle of the icy wind outside the cave.

"What?" she finally managed, her voice hoarse. "Talor and I?"

The seer nodded, her sly smile widening. "It's the only way."

"Then your people are doomed," Talor spoke up, his voice icy. "For there is no way I will ever bind myself to a Serpent woman."

Old Murdina's smile faded, and her smoke grey eyes narrowed. "Careful, lad. You could do far worse than Mor. I've seen the way you look at her. Your body wants her, even if your stubborn ways prevent you from admitting it to yourself."

Mor's belly twisted as she watched Talor's face turn to stone. The thought of being handfasted to her was abhorrent to him; he did not even bother to hide his disgust at the very notion.

"Save your advice for the feeble-minded," he snarled at the seer. "I have no use for it."

With that, Talor turned on his heel and strode from the cave without a backward glance.

A heartbeat later Mor moved to follow him. She could not let Talor leave. He was her only chance at weaving peace.

"Stop, Mor." Old Murdina's sharp command forestalled her.

Whipping around, Mor fixed the crone with a baleful look. "You handled that well," she snapped. "Couldn't you have broached the subject more softly?"

Old Murdina croaked a laugh. "There's little point in that, lass. Talor mac Donnel prefers plain speech."

"Well, he didn't like what you had to say."

"It came as a shock to him, aye."

Mor stepped back, glancing over her shoulder at the mouth of the cave. "I need to go after him ... he has to see sense."

"Nothing you say will make any difference," the bandruí replied, her tone serious now. "Let him go. If Talor agrees to wed you ... or to aid you in your quest for peace ... it must be a decision he makes for himself."

Chapter Thirteen

A Warrior's Death

CATHAL MAC CALUM slammed his fist onto the table. Pain shot up his arm and splinters drove into his knuckles, yet he was too incensed to care.

"How is it possible that they could have just disappeared," he railed at the group of warriors that surrounded him on the platform. "They won't have just vanished into a fairy mound. They will be hiding somewhere ... and you were supposed to find them."

"The snow has made it difficult," Tormud replied. He was the only warrior bold enough to respond, especially considering the chieftain's enraged state. The rest held their tongues, their gazes wary and faces taut. None of them wanted to fail Cathal, and yet they all had. "It has covered their tracks ... they could be anywhere."

Cathal spat out a curse and stormed from the platform, shoving Tormud aside as he did so. He could not bear to look at their faces. He could not believe they were all so incompetent—especially Tormud, who was supposed to know this isle well. Even Old Murdina had been of no use to him. When he had been to visit her earlier in the day, the bandruí had merely looked at him with a smirk that had made him want to take a stick to her.

Ignoring the folk that filled the feasting hall, he stalked across the floor, kicking a dog out of the way as he went. The hound yelped and slunk away, but Cathal ignored it. Instead, he left the broch, welcoming the gust of icy air that hit his face the moment he stepped outside.

Another snowy dusk was settling. Snow gusted in, carried by a biting north wind. It was a vicious night to be outdoors, a night when those without shelter would surely freeze.

Maybe the cold has claimed them both.

The thought brought Cathal mixed reactions: a surge of vindictive pleasure at the thought of the Eagle warrior lying frozen in a gully, and a knife-blade of grief under his ribcage at the image of his daughter's lifeless eyes staring up into the sky.

Fury swiftly followed, seizing him by the throat.

How could Mor do this to me?

Cathal stormed down the steps, nearly slipping on the sheet of ice that had frozen over them. He then made his way across the yard and climbed another set of steps, these even steeper and more perilous than the last, and reached the top of the high wall that encircled the fort. On a clear day, it afforded a view of the rocky shoreline to the south, where Old Murdina dwelt in that damp cave, and the craggy headland beyond. But tonight, the snow obscured everything.

The wind was strong up here, buffeting him. Cathal had been so caught up in a rage that he left the broch without a fur cloak. As such, the wind clawed at his exposed skin, driving sharp needles into his flesh.

Cathal welcomed the sensation, for it pushed out the seething rage that had nowhere to go.

Walking to the edge of the wall, he clenched his hands by his side and tried to control the anger that clawed its way up his throat. He wanted to kill, to maim. He wanted to howl into the wind at the cruelty of fate.

After a few moments Cathal realized he was not alone.

Breathing heavily, he turned his gaze right, at where a broad-shouldered figure swathed in fur watched him. Despite his injuries, Artair had followed him up here.

"Here." His brother handed him a cloak. "I thought you'd need this."

Cathal took the cloak without a word of thanks and slung it around his shoulders. Immediately, the biting cold retreated just a little, allowing the furnace of his fury to warm him once more.

"They've all deserted me, Artair," he ground out finally, his gaze sweeping south. "I arrived on these shores with three children. None are left."

"Mor could still be alive," his brother rumbled.

"It doesn't matter if she still breathes," Cathal growled back. "She's dead to me now." He glanced back at Artair then. Illuminated by the light of a brazier, his brother's face looked tired and haggard. Those injuries he had sustained in the siege of Balintur pained him still. Cathal wondered if Artair would ever fully recover from them. "Why did she do it? Why did she betray me?"

Artair shook his head, his gaze shadowing. "I'm as mystified as you," he admitted softly. He stepped closer to Cathal then, and the two brothers stood shoulder to shoulder as the wind buffeted their backs. "You don't think she fell for him, do you?"

Cathal's mouth twisted. "If she did, it was the swiftest love affair I've ever witnessed. Mor didn't spend any time alone with that Eagle bastard ... did she?"

"I never saw her do so."

Silence fell between them for a long moment, and when Cathal finally glanced at his brother, he saw Artair staring out into the snowy evening. "They can't have survived out there," he murmured.

Cathal grunted. "You forget, Talor mac Donnel is one of the Eagle. He knows these lands. If there was a hiding place, he's sure to have found it."

Another silence drew out between the brothers, and when Artair finally broke it, his voice was quiet, cautious. "Are you still set on remaining upon this isle, Cathal?"

Cathal clenched his jaw before replying, "Aye ... more than ever."

"There are still close to two hundred of us within the walls of Dun Ringill," Artair replied, his voice carefully neutral. "Two hundred men and women who would follow you anywhere ... you know that."

"Aye," Cathal growled. "What of it?"

"You may have lost Dunchadh, Tamhas ... and Mor ... but you still have the rest of us," Artair continued. "You hold our lives in your hands. Are you sure you want to see the end to our people on this rock?"

Cathal cut his brother a sharp look. "What makes you think it will be our end?"

Artair exhaled sharply, anger splintering his usual reserve. Artair was very different to Cathal. The Serpent chieftain knew he had a fiery temper, that his brother had always been the cool, level-headed one. "They outnumber us now," Artair pointed out.

"It doesn't matter. We are better fighters. We can wait them out inside these walls."

"Can we? The walls aren't the problem ... how long do you think the gates will hold out against a sustained attack? If they encircle us, they'll hammer at our defenses until they get through ... and then we'll be massacred."

"Aye, but it will be a warrior's death for all of us," Cathal shot back. "We won't slink away like cowards."

"None of us are craven," Artair countered, exasperated now. "None of us have anything to prove. But as chieftain, you have the power to give us back a future ... to take us from these shores to a new home."

"Enough," Cathal snarled, his patience snapping. He had come up onto the wall to be alone with his rage—not to be nagged. His brother had just succeeded in fueling his ire further. All this talk of fleeing like beaten hounds made his gut twist. "There is nowhere else for us, Artair," he continued. "We came here as a last resort. The mainland is lost to us. We make our stand here. There is no other choice."

Artair did not reply immediately. Instead, he let the wind howl between them for a few moments, let the blizzard consume them in a white world, before he answered. And when he did, his voice was rough with anger. "There's always a choice, Cathal. Always."

Chapter Fourteen

Making Choices

MOR SET OUT for the hunter's hut at first light.

Old Murdina had convinced her not to attempt the journey in the darkness, especially as another snowstorm had howled in, blanketing the world in white. Instead, Mor shared a light supper of oatcakes and hard cheese before wrapping herself up in her fur cloak near the glowing hearth. It was cold, damp, and drafty inside the cave, and the ground was rock-hard. Mor had not thought she would manage to sleep at all, yet she had—such had been her exhaustion. But with the first blush of dawn, she had risen, bid the seer farewell, and set off east toward the mountains.

"The Gods have spoken. If you want peace, then a union with Talor mac Donnel is the only way," the bandruí had reminded her. The crone had shuffled to the mouth of her cave to see her off. "Only then will an alliance be formed between our people."

Mor had acknowledged the comment with a curt nod, before she pulled her cloak tightly about her and emerged into the freezing dawn.

The snow still fell lightly now, although the wind had died. The morning felt eerily quiet.

I hope he returned to the hut. Mor struggled up the slope and headed toward the brow of the first snow-covered hill. *He could have just gone back to his people.*

The thought made Mor's belly tighten. Upon awaking, she had told herself that despite his anger the night before, Talor would see sense once he calmed down. He would be waiting for her at the hut—and this time would be ready to talk.

He'll be there, she assured herself.

Mor feared she might not find the valley again. Fortunately, she had paid attention the day before when they had traveled to Old Murdina's cave, and had noted that for the most part, Talor had led her directly west, without too many detours north or south. As such, she kept her course steady in the opposite direction.

Once the mountains loomed before her, it was easier to get her bearings. She remembered the shape of one of them, thrusting skyward like a shark fin. The valley where they had sheltered lay at the bottom of it, with the hut at the far end.

The sight of the small dwelling made relief crash over Mor in a great wave. She had been traveling all morning, and all the while the snow had silently fallen. She was tired now, and her feet and hands were numb. Old Murdina had given her some more oatcakes to take with her, and she still had a bladder of water.

She wondered how Talor was faring. He would not have eaten anything since the day before and would likely be weak with hunger.

But when Mor ducked into the low entrance of the hut, she found the interior empty. She moved over to the hearth and checked the ashes there. They were stone cold; no one had been here since they had left it the day before.

Talor had not returned as she had hoped.

Sitting back on her haunches, Mor spat out a curse. She should have realized the man had no honor. She had saved his life, and this was how he repaid her?

A chill washed over her then, and her skin prickled. She suddenly felt like a complete goose. She had been too trusting. It had been idiocy to take him into her confidence.

The memory of how his face had twisted, when Old Murdina had made her divination, made her skin prickle with humiliation. The thought had revolted him.

Suddenly, she questioned everything. Although the seer thought differently, maybe the fascination she'd had with him from beginning—that pull, like a moth to a flame—had all been on her side only.

Mor breathed another curse before raking a hand over her face.

What now?

Her choices were limited. Wearily, she heaved herself up off the ground and exited the hut. After trudging through the snow since dawn to reach her destination, the last thing she wanted to do was continue walking. There was enough peat left for her to build another fire, and she desperately wanted to rest for a while.

But Talor would not help her; something had to be done. She could not hide out here in the mountains and pretend nothing had happened. Panic now churned through her. This was all her doing; she had taken this responsibility on herself. No one had forced her on this path.

Desperation twisted her belly. Mor fisted her hands at her sides, forcing down the spiraling panic. She had to act. If Talor would not aid her, maybe others would.

Despite everything, she was as committed to peace as she had ever been. It was too late to turn back now. She would take this to the very end, wherever that led her.

Squaring her shoulders, Mor cast one final glance back at the hut, and then she turned and retraced her steps down the snow-covered valley.

Talor trudged up the incline and drew to a halt.

Even covered in three feet of snow, he knew this valley instantly.

A deep, steep sided vale, studded with great towering stacks of stone, spread out before him. The tors thrust up out of the snow, stark against the surrounding blanket of white. Casting his gaze over the valley, Talor reflected on all the bloodshed that had taken place in this spot. The Valley of the Tors, for that was its name, marked the boundary between The Boar and The Eagle. Many battles had occurred here, the most recent of which had been the violent skirmish between the two tribes last summer. It had occurred just days before the Cruthini invaded. Fina had lost her entire patrol in that fight and fallen prisoner to Varar mac Urcal.

Talor's mouth twisted at the memory. Much had happened since then.

It seemed like years ago, not last summer.

Breathing heavily, Talor decided to rest for a short while. He sagged against one of the tors, taking strength from its bulk. After leaving Mor and the seer the night before, he had traveled down the coast. There were more caves, harder to reach and far less comfortable, farther south. Talor had sheltered in one of them for the rest of the night before pressing on with the dawn.

Walking gave him plenty of time to think, to mull over the events of the past few days. However, when his thoughts shifted to Mor, guilt arrowed through him.

You shouldn't have walked out on her.

Talor ground his teeth and shoved aside his needling conscience.

I had to ... going to that cave was a waste of time.

The bandruí's proclamation still rang in his ears, shadowing him as he trudged south. It reminded him of the prediction that Ailene had made over a month earlier at Mid-Winter Fire. She had been so excited that evening, seeking him out as he took up his place upon the wall for the night watch.

"The bloodshed will end," his cousin had told him, her blue eyes shining with joy. "The bones speak of a union between The Serpent and The Eagle."

Talor had curled his lip at her words and rudely turned his back upon her. The notion had been ridiculous.

And yet Old Murdina's divination had been uncomfortably close to Ailene's.

Talor shook his head, attempting to dislodge the thoughts that plagued him. He had done the right thing in walking away from that cave, in distancing himself from that Serpent woman. Now he just had to reach An Teanga, where his cousin Fina resided. Once he reached Varar and Fina, he would be safe. He would be able to rest up, fill his belly, and rebuild his strength to fight the enemy once more.

The day drew out, and exhaustion dragged at him. He had slaked his thirst with some snow, but his belly ached in hunger. His head was starting to spin now, and he could feel weakness filtering through his limbs. Talor needed to reach The Boar stronghold by the day's end. But it was an ambitious plan; he risked collapsing before arriving at his destination.

Talor heaved in a deep breath, stubbornness forcing him on. He shoved himself away from the tor he had been leaning against and staggered down the hill. He would not be beaten. He had managed to cheat death a few times over the past days. He could not let it be for nothing.

But halfway down the hill, Talor's legs suddenly gave out from under him.

He tumbled forward, unable to save himself, and rolled down the bank, landing on a crust of fresh snow at the bottom of the valley.

Talor groaned, rolling over and glaring up at the pale sky. It had stopped snowing for the moment, but he could see that the light was fading; dusk approached. He was still too far away from An Teanga. His chest constricted as he realized that he would not reach it by nightfall.

Still refusing to be beaten, Talor heaved himself to his feet. He had rarely ever felt so weak. The beatings, coupled with the cold and the lack of food, were finally starting to take their toll. Fear curled up within him then. He risked collapsing out here in the wilderness. And if it snowed again, his body would be covered, only to be discovered when the spring thaw came.

The grisly thought spurred him on.

He had only gone a few feet across the wide valley floor, when a shout drew his attention. Talor's head snapped up.

The sound had come from the south, and he craned his neck, his gaze scanning the tor-studded hillside. It came to a rest upon the dark outlines of warriors and ponies against the sky. A large band had halted at the crest of the next hill.

Relief suffused Talor, the emotion so strong that his vision misted. He lifted an arm and waved, for he knew, even without seeing their faces, who these people were.

The war band, a carpet of spears that bristled against the sky, advanced down the hillside. And as they drew closer, Talor spied many familiar faces. The warriors were dressed for battle, and carried weapons and shields. Despite the freezing weather, some of the men went bare-chested, their chests and arms smeared with blue woad; while many of the women dressed scantily in short leather or plaid skirts, with leather bands binding their breasts. Their only concessions to the cold were the fur cloaks each warrior wore around their shoulders and heavy fur boots.

His cousin Fina was among the group. She stalked toward him now, her heart-shaped face rigid with concern.

Talor realized then that she had been the one to call out, the one who had spied him first.

"Talor!" Fina rushed at him. "What are you doing out here?" Her iron-grey eyes narrowed then, as she took in the state of him. "The Reaper's Cods," she muttered. "What happened to you?"

Talor attempted a cocky smile but failed. He was so exhausted that it was difficult to appear otherwise.

"It's a long tale," he rasped. "But give me some food and drink, and let me catch my breath, and I will tell you it all."

Chapter Fifteen

Stubborn

THE BOAR MADE camp in the Valley of the Tors. Night was almost upon them, and the valley made as good a place as any to settle down for the evening.

Huddled over a brazier, where a lump of peat burned hot, Talor let out a long sigh. He had forgotten what it was like to feel warm. But inside this tent, with soft fur beneath his bare feet, he almost felt his old self again.

Almost.

"I don't know whether to be impressed or horrified." A deep male voice rumbled. Varar mac Urcal, chieftain of The Boar, reclined upon a pile of furs a few feet away. Despite his relaxed posture, leaning back as he listened to Talor's tale, Varar possessed a predatory stillness. Talor had rarely met a man as dangerous as Varar, or as brave.

Talor huffed a laugh, before he shifted his attention to the small woman wearing a scowl who stood a few feet away, watching him, hands on hips. "You've done some daft things in your life ... but that was by far the stupidest," Fina growled out the words. "It's only by the grace of the Gods that you are still breathing. Not that you deserve to be."

Talor winced at her harsh words. Fina was never one to hold back. And, in the wake of everything that had happened, he now agreed with her.

If he could go back in time, he would not have set out on this path. It was idiotic; he saw that now. But at the time he had been blinded by grief. The sorrow was still there, simmering away in the pit of his belly, a constant reminder of what he had lost.

"The behavior of Cathal's daughter surprises me," Varar spoke up, shattering the tense silence that had settled over the tent. "I find it hard to believe that she actually wants peace."

Fina snorted, making it clear that she agreed with him.

"The woman is a half-wit," Talor replied with a sneer. "She betrayed her own people on a whim. She can't go back to them now, not without punishment."

Even to his own ears, the words sounded harsh. Guilt rose once more within Talor, but he hastily crushed it. He decided he would not tell Varar and Fina about their disastrous visit to the bandruí.

Bitterness soured his mouth at the memory. Old Murdina's divination had made fury wash over him, drowning all reason. How dare the crone suggest such a thing? She had known he was attracted to Mor, that his body wanted her. Aye, he found the Cruthini woman striking, an exotic beauty whose nearness caused his pulse to race and his groin to tighten.

But that meant nothing. He would not wed a Serpent.

Images rose unbidden then, of their fight inside the hut.

Talor had deliberately provoked Mor, and if he had not been hurting from his injuries, he might have enjoyed fighting her. She was quick, strong, and knew how to fight dirty—but uninjured he could have bested her.

He imagined the scene. Her spread-eagled beneath him on the cold, hard floor of that hunters' hut, his body pressed flush against hers as she glared up at him, fury and defiance in those moss green eyes. He envisioned the long length of her body, imagined grinding his hips against hers and the softness of those magnificent breasts thrust up against him.

Talor's groin hardened, responding to the heated images. Clenching his jaw, and glad that his crouched position hid his arousal, Talor banished the lusty thoughts. This wasn't helping.

"I'm surprised you didn't go straight back to Dun Ringill and try to slit Cathal's throat again," Fina said, shattering Talor's introspection. "It's not like you to give up so easily."

Talor pulled a face. "I swore Mor an oath that I wouldn't," he admitted.

That got both their attention. Varar raised an eyebrow, and Fina tilted her head, her gaze narrowing. "Why did you do that?"

"She forced it out of me ... it was either that or freeze to death."

"And does she know that an Eagle always keeps his oaths?" Fina asked after a pause.

Talor huffed a wry laugh. "She does now."

Another silence settled inside the tent. Beyond, Talor caught the snatches of conversation in the camp, as the war band settled down for the night. The warriors of the united tribes were moving against Dun Ringill. Talor knew that the attack had been coming. However, his disappearance had moved things forward. Despite the heavy snows, which made travel and fighting difficult, they would attack The Eagle stronghold at last.

Warmth ignited in Talor's belly at the thought. Snow or not—it was time.

Fina had told him that a rider arrived in An Teanga the day before. The Boar war band was to meet the rest of the army in a shallow vale just east of Dun Ringill. From there they would launch a siege.

Now that the bulge in his breeches had subsided, Talor sat back on his heels and ran a hand over his tired face. He had filled his belly with buttered oatcakes and boiled eggs, washing it down with a cup of ale. All he needed now was to rest, and by morning he would be ready to face the world again.

Indeed, the world appeared a happier, brighter place the following morning. The snow had ceased for a short while, and the sky turned pale blue as the first blush of dawn faded.

Talor stepped outside the tent and stretched his stiff and aching limbs. A good night's sleep had revived him considerably—as had the anticipation of taking back Dun Ringill for his people. He could not wait to set foot inside the broch once more, to look out over Loch Slapin with the sea-breeze on his face.

Nonetheless, Talor still winced as he massaged a bruised muscle in his shoulder. What he needed was to soak in a tub of steaming water and let the aches and pains of the last few days seep from him. But that was not going to happen anytime soon.

Around him Boar warriors were starting to pack up the sea of hide tents that carpeted the bottom of the valley. Deciding to make himself useful too, Talor turned and began helping other men take down the large chieftain's tent. A group of ponies followed the war band, laden down with rolls of hide and poles for erecting the tents. There was no camping without tents under the sky this time of year. And if they were going to mount a campaign against Dun Ringill, they would need time. They could not let the cold defeat them, before they brought The Serpent down.

Rolling up the last of the furs that carpeted the floor of Varar's tent, Talor inhaled the aroma of baking oatcakes. Following the moreish smell, he reached a group of warriors gathered around a large central fire pit, where women were cooking batches of oatcakes. One of the women was Morag, Varar's elder sister. Her bairn, who was barely a few moons old now, hung in a sling on her back. The lad already had a thick thatch of dark hair, and his chubby hands waved in the chill morning air as his mother expertly flipped yet another batch of cooked oatcakes onto a platter. She then handed it, with a smile, to Fina.

Thanking her, Fina moved away from the fire pit and headed toward Talor. "You're looking better this morning," she greeted her cousin. Fina then thrust the platter at him. "Go on, help yourself … careful though … they're hot."

Talor grinned at Fina before taking a large handful of cakes. She was right, they scorched his fingers, but he welcomed the heat. Although the sun was out this morning, there was no warmth in it at all; his breath clouded in front of him.

"You had me worried when we came across you yesterday," his cousin continued. Fina helped herself to just one cake before passing the platter on. She then turned, fixing Talor with a penetrating gaze that he knew well. "You do realize you were close to collapse?"

Talor's grin faded, and he nodded. The fact had not escaped him.

He took a big bite of oatcake, chewing vigorously. Fresh off the griddle, these were delicious; although he liked them best slathered with butter. After days without a meal, he was not about to be fussy. He noted then that his cousin, who usually had a robust appetite, was nibbling delicately at the oatcake she held. Her face was pale this morning, and she looked a bit peaky.

"Is something wrong?" Talor asked with a frown. "Are you unwell, Fina?"

Fina's mouth curved. "Nothing is lost on you, is it, cousin?"

When Talor did not answer, she sighed. "You might as well know … I am with bairn."

Talor's gaze widened. "Really?"

"I've been feeling strange for a few days," she replied, lowering her voice so that they were not overheard. "My moon flow never arrived last month, and when I started to feel queasy, I went to see the healer. Eachann confirmed it."

Talor cut a glance over to where Varar mac Urcal stood on the opposite side of the fire pit. He was deep in discussion with one of his warriors and did not look their way.

"Does Varar know?"

"Of course he does," Fina replied with a toss of her head. "We keep nothing from each other."

"And he's happy for you to come on this campaign?" Protectiveness rose within Talor, as did a surge of anger toward Varar. Fina was a warrior to be sure, but now that she carried a bairn, she needed to be protected.

Fina rolled her eyes. "Of course he isn't. But he can't stop me from fighting." She held up a hand then, forestalling his objection. "And don't you start either. I've already had this argument with Varar many times. I'm carrying a child, but that doesn't mean I'm useless. We need every warrior at hand for the siege. I will not stand back and watch everyone else fight. That is my final word on the subject."

Talor's gaze narrowed. He swallowed the urge to argue with her, although irritation now boiled within him. Fina could be so pigheaded at times. It was a trait that ran in their family—passed down to the mac Muin brothers from their strong-willed father. Once they set their mind on something, they would not be swayed.

But sometimes being so stubborn got you into serious trouble. It had been a hard lesson for Talor, but the events of late had taught him a few things. If he survived the days to come, he would be more cautious in future before rashly throwing himself into situations.

Talor's chest tightened as he realized he had Mor to thank for that.

Chapter Sixteen

A Friend of Yours

IT WAS A slow journey north. Weighed down by weapons and supplies, the company of ponies, with many warriors traveling on foot, struggled through the deep snow. The sky remained clear during the journey, which made it easier to keep watch on the horizon.

Despite that Fina had tried to give Talor her pony—asserting that he would heal faster if he rested—he had insisted on traveling on foot.

He was hardly going to take a pony from a pregnant woman. Fina had tried to argue with him, telling him that he would be no good to them in battle if he was weak and wounded. But Talor had still declined. He was feeling a lot stronger now. And he enjoyed the walking; it took his mind off things. When he focused on putting one foot in front of the other, he could distract himself from his circling thoughts.

Even so, as the day wore on, he found himself wondering about Mor.

He had been dismissive of her in front of Varar and
Fina, yet the woman was never far from his thoughts.
Where had she gone after leaving Old Murdina? She had
not chased him, so he guessed she would have remained
overnight in the bandruí's cave. But after that? Perhaps
she had returned to the hunters' hut. Had she expected
to find him there? Of course, she would be sorely
disappointed if she had. Maybe she had returned to Dun
Ringill to face her father instead?

Talor frowned as he considered this. Would she take
such a risk?

He had not known Mor for very long, and in reality
did not understand the woman at all, but he sensed that
she was not the type to hide from conflict. Now that
Talor had abandoned her, she would likely decide to face
her father and deal with the consequences.

She would suffer because of him.

Talor's belly clenched at the prospect. *It was her
choice to free you*, he reminded himself, irritated by the
turn of his thoughts. *You owe her nothing*.

The words were true enough, but in the stark light of
day, they felt hollow. The fact remained that Mor had
saved his life, and he had refused to help her.

An image flashed before him then, of Mor staring at
him after his outburst in the bandruí's cave. He had seen
the hurt in her eyes.

He might have felt justified, but he had acted badly all
the same.

She's not your responsibility, he reminded himself,
irritation flaring into anger. *Stop thinking about her*.

Talor gave his head a shake and quickened his step
through the soft, powdery snow. His gaze fixed north,
and for the rest of the afternoon he focused only on
reaching his destination.

Dusk was settling when they arrived at the camp of
the warriors of the united tribes at last.

Talor paused on the edge of the shallow valley that
stretched before them. The sight took his breath away: a
great carpet of tents and glowing fires filled the valley. It

made their numbers seem huge. Gazing at the army, Talor reckoned that they were at least four hundred strong. They had brought warriors from every corner of the isle, emptying out Dun Grianan and Dun Ardtreck, as well as many of the smaller settlements to the north. They would launch everything they had at Dun Ringill for the siege.

This was the turning point. The coming days would decide the fate of them all.

"An impressive sight, isn't it?"

Varar's voice roused Talor from his scrutiny. He cut The Boar warrior a glance and favored him with a grim smile. "A welcome one indeed," he replied. "Our numbers are bigger than I expected."

Varar nodded. "I was worried after Balintur that we would be too weakened, but the people of this isle are hard to crush, it seems."

Talor's gaze shifted once more to the glowing encampment before him. They had already set up a watch around the perimeter; a line of guttering pitch torches formed a protective circle on all sides of the valley. "I wish Bonnie was here to see this," he murmured. "Battle was in her blood. She loved a good scrap."

"Then she died how she would have chosen," Varar replied, his voice lowering. "The lass fell too young, but none of us who choose a warrior's life know when the end will come. I'm sure Bonnie was aware of the risks she took. She will be looking down on you now though ... be sure of that."

Talor raised an eyebrow, fixing Varar with a wry look. "Really?"

"Don't look so skeptical," The Boar chastised him. "Every time I go into battle, I can feel my father watching over me. Urcal mac Wrad loved getting blood on his hands." Varar's gaze shadowed then. "Unfortunately, my father didn't die a warrior's death ... illness took him from us. He would have been bitter about that."

At the mention of Varar's father, Talor thought of his own, and as he did so, his belly tightened.

Donnel would not be happy with his errant son. He was not looking forward to facing him.

"Idiot!" Donnel stepped close to Talor, going nose to nose with him. "If your face didn't look like you've been trampled by a herd of goats, I'd blacken your eye."

Talor held his father's gaze, unwavering. He had barely set foot inside the camp when he had seen his kin approach. Joy and relief had mingled with dread at the sight of them. Then, he had left Varar's side and stridden toward the small group. There were some meetings that could not be put off.

Around them, many of the camp rose from their firesides and approached the newcomers, gazes alight with interest. Talor knew they were shocked to see him return to them.

Eithni stood a couple of feet behind her husband, with Talor's half-sister, Eara, at her side. They stared at Talor, their eyes glittering with tears of joy at seeing him alive. But his father merely looked angry.

Talor welcomed his fury; he almost wished his father would lash out, would bust his nose or split his lip.

He deserved it.

"Because of you, the army has mobilized early," Donnel continued. "Because of you, we're going to lay siege to Dun Ringill in a blizzard."

"I'm sorry," he said finally, letting his father's anger wash over him. "I shouldn't have left as I did. It was selfish and rash."

Donnel drew back slightly, his gaze widening. "What? You're not going to make some excuse? You're not going to argue with me?"

Talor shook his head. "No, I'm not."

Donnel's gaze narrowed. "What's wrong with you?"

"He's clearly exhausted and injured, Donnel," Eithni spoke up. Her voice held an uncharacteristic sharp edge as she addressed her husband. "You can tear your son to pieces later ... I should check him first."

Donnel glanced back at his wife and cast her an exasperated look. "You can tend to his wounds soon enough," he replied, "but there are other, more urgent matters to be addressed first."

Talor tensed at these words. He had hoped his father would leave well enough alone once he admitted he had been at fault, but it seemed Donnel had no intention of doing so.

His father's eyes were a dark storm-grey as his gaze fused with his son's once more. "We've been camped here since yesterday morning," he said after a pause, "and at dusk we had a visitor."

Donnel broke off there, and Talor shifted his attention to where three men approached: Galan mac Muin, Tadhg mac Fortrenn, and Wid mac Manus. All three chieftains wore grim expressions.

A chill feathered down Talor's spine, before he glanced back at his father. "A visitor?"

Donnel's mouth thinned. "Aye ... a *friend* of yours." When Talor frowned, confused, his father continued. "Cathal mac Calum's daughter is now our captive."

Chapter Seventeen

That is My Fate

TALOR FOLLOWED THE chieftains into the tent, his gaze arrowing immediately to the tall, proud figure that stood in the center of it. Hands bound behind her, Mor watched the men enter. But her inscrutable expression slipped just a little when she saw who accompanied them.

Their gazes fused. For a moment Talor felt his surroundings slip away. All that existed was Mor's long-lashed cool-green eyes drawing him into their depths. She mesmerized him, as she had the first time they locked gazes in Dun Ringill.

He realized then with a jolt that although he had known Mor only a short while, he had actually missed her over the past day.

How was it possible? He had stridden from that cave without a backward glance, but, somehow, Mor had gotten under his skin.

The realization was not something that pleased him.

"Look who arrived with the dusk." Wid of the Wolf's voice was a low rumble as he approached the brazier that glowed in the center of the tent. Wid glowered across at their captive. "Lucky for you, he did."

The hard edge to the Wolf chieftain's voice made Talor tense, as did the threatening undertone. He cast a glance then at his uncle Galan. Likewise, The Eagle chieftain was frowning, his dark brows knitted together. His mouth compressed as he returned Talor's stare. "None of us believed her story," he admitted. "If you hadn't returned to us by dawn, we were going to drag this Serpent out before the walls of Dun Ringill and make an example of her."

These words alarmed Talor, although he did his best to hide his reaction. He should not care what happened to Mor. After all, she was the enemy. But the thought of her being executed made something twist deep inside his chest.

He glanced over at Varar. The Boar chieftain's expression was guarded. He had joined them for this meeting, but he was holding his tongue, preferring to let Talor take the lead.

"So, she was telling the truth then?" Tadhg of The Wolf asked. The big bearded warrior was watching Talor, his gaze narrowed. "She helped you escape Dun Ringill?"

Talor did not answer immediately. Instead, he glanced to Mor. This was his chance. If he truly hated this woman, now was his opportunity to drive the blade in and twist it hard. One word from him and she would die at dawn. Mor stared back at him, her gaze level and fearless. She would not plead; she was too proud for that.

"Aye," Talor admitted finally. "She doesn't lie. I tried to kill Cathal and failed. He had me beaten and hung me up outside the broch to freeze to death in the snow. But that evening Mor freed me, and together we fled Dun Ringill. We hid in a hunters' hut inland."

"And how was it you came to be separated?" Galan asked. "Why did Mor travel here on her own while you arrive a day later with The Boar war band?"

Talor tensed further at this question. His uncle was no fool; he could tell there was something that his nephew was leaving out.

It dawned upon Talor then that Mor had not told them of their trip to see the bandruí. He went still as he realized the implication of this. Perhaps she feared the seer's prediction would enrage the chieftains. Likewise, Talor did not feel like revealing what Old Murdina had told them. He had not mentioned the meeting to Varar and Fina, and he felt even more reluctant to say anything now in front of the others.

He wished to forget her words altogether. The idea of allying his people with the invaders still soured his belly.

"We argued the following day," Talor said after a long pause. It was the same excuse he had used with Varar and Fina. "After that we went our separate ways."

Galan watched him for a moment, before he glanced at Mor. "Your stories align," his uncle admitted grudgingly. "But I still don't understand why you would make a sacrifice of yourself, lass. You must have known what would happen if you came here?"

Mor drew in a slow, deep breath. When she spoke, her voice was low and held a husky edge that sent a jolt of arousal straight to Talor's groin. The Hag curse this woman, even her voice moved him.

"I want peace between our tribes," she said, her attention never leaving Galan. "I knew that I was breaking with my own people when I freed Talor. That sacrifice should mean something. I'm here to build a bridge between us. Why can't we live together upon this isle? There is enough space for all of us."

Wid barked a harsh laugh. "You ask this of us now? After leaving a trail of carnage in your wake?"

Around him Galan and Tadhg frowned, while Varar nodded in agreement with Wid. His people had suffered greatly because of The Serpent; he would not forget that easily.

Mor squared her shoulders. "Launching an attack was my father's chosen path ... not mine. I wish for our peoples to share The Winged Isle."

"That's only because we have you surrounded," Varar said, a threatening edge to his voice. "You know your people are doomed."

Mor stared back at The Boar chieftain, her features tightening. "We can always make a fresh start," she said hoarsely. "You just have to want it."

A brittle silence fell inside the tent.

Across the brazier Tadhg mac Fortrenn folded his brawny arms across a broad chest. "So, how were you intending to achieve peace, lass?" he rumbled. "Surely, you didn't think speaking to us would be enough?"

Mor's attention shifted to the big warrior, and Talor saw determination flare in her eyes once more. "There will be talks before the battle," she replied without a trace of hesitation. It appeared she had thought all of this through. "Take me out with you, and let me speak to my father. Let me see if I can talk him around. Maybe I can convince him to negotiate. And if he agrees to lay down arms ... will you spare our people's lives? Will you let us stay here?"

"There will be no negotiation ... we will *never* share this isle with you." Wid's harsh voice shattered the moment of stillness that followed Mor's words. Talor knew that the past year had taken a great toll on Wid mac Manus. He had lost a son and developed a bitter shell in the aftermath. The man before Talor now was vastly different to the good-natured, laughing warrior he remembered from his childhood. "We're going to bring your people down."

Mor stared back at the Wolf chieftain, a nerve flickering under one eye. It was the only sign of the turmoil that now churned within her. "Surely, you wouldn't slaughter those who willingly surrender?"

Watching Mor, Talor felt a pang of sympathy for her. It was an impossible, hopeless situation, and yet she was ready to confront it. He had always thought of himself as foolishly reckless, but this woman outdid him.

Galan let out a sharp breath. "I've no wish to share The Winged Isle with these Cruthini," he admitted, "But I will not strike down those who do not raise arms against me." He shifted his attention to the other chieftains. "What say the rest of you? Shall we take her out with us to talk to Cathal? Shall we give them one last chance? If they surrender, we can then decide what to do with them."

Varar scowled. "This is Cathal's last opportunity to back down," he growled. "There will be no others."

Next to The Boar chieftain, Tadhg heaved in a deep breath before replying, "I agree."

Wid glowered back at Galan, clearly angry that The Eagle chieftain was prepared to compromise. A heavy pause stretched out, before Wid spat on the ground before him. "Very well ... let her humiliate herself ... let Cathal prove himself a worthless dog once more, and then let us get on with the battle. But even if they surrender, I will *never* share my homeland with that filth!"

Mor's expression darkened then, the first sign that any of them had angered her. A tense silence fell, before Talor shifted restlessly. "Are we done here?" he asked, meeting his uncle's eye.

Galan nodded, splintering the hostile atmosphere. "For now."

"Can I have a few moments alone with the prisoner?" Talor asked.

Galan cocked his head, before he shared a glance with the other chieftains. "I can't see how that will hurt," he said finally. "But make it quick."

"Aye," Tadhg rumbled. "No one else is allowed in here tonight ... I have warriors encircling the tent.

The four chieftains departed without another word, leaving Talor and Mor alone.

They stood in silence for a few moments. Mor's face had gone taut, her eyes burning. She was still fuming over Wid's comments. Tension rippled off her in waves.

"You shouldn't be here." When Talor spoke, he was surprised to hear the rough edge to his voice.

Mor's mouth thinned in response.

"I thought you were level-headed," Talor said, taking a step toward her. "You should leave the acts of idiocy to me."

"I considered my options, Talor mac Donnel," she replied, "and this was my best one." She paused there, her gaze narrowing. "Do you really think I would have gone home to my father?"

Talor frowned. "I thought you had. He might have shown mercy on you. You're his daughter after all."

"But then all hope at bridging the gulf between our peoples would be lost. I'm the only one who can stop this bloodshed."

"You take a lot upon yourself," Talor replied, his tone softening. "Do you really think that one woman can prevent all this? It's like holding back the tide, Mor. Some things are impossible to stop."

He moved closer to her then. The green of her eyes seemed to intensify as he drew nearer; the glow of the brazier she stood before flickered in their depths.

"I have to try." Her voice hitched slightly, revealing that her shield was starting to slip. "I'm doing this for my people. Even if I fail, I can't keep silent anymore." Her throat bobbed. "When my brothers ... Dunchadh and Tamhas ... fell, they took a piece of me with them. I'm heart sore and world weary, Talor. I just want an end to all of this."

Her words made Talor pause a moment. The grief within her writhed close to the surface now; her eyes gleamed with tears. For the first time Talor saw this invasion from her perspective. The Serpent had arrived upon these shores with high hopes for the future, but with each passing moon those dreams were turning to dust.

Mor had paid a high price for a new life upon The Winged Isle.

Talor could not help it. He shifted even nearer, so that they stood barely a foot apart now. He could feel the warmth of her body, could hear the soft whisper of her breathing. She stared at him, her full lips parting as she reacted to his nearness.

Talor drew in a steadying breath. Did she feel that too? This irresistible pull. Whenever he stood too close to her, he found it hard to breathe. His pulse accelerated.

Neither of them spoke then—Mor simply stared at him.

Without considering his actions, Talor reached out, tangling his hands in her thick auburn hair. He dug his fingers deep, shifting closer still and splaying his hands across the back of her scalp. With her own hands bound behind her, she was trapped.

Wordlessly, Talor tipped Mor's head back, exposing her neck. Without pausing to consider his actions, he then dipped his head and grazed the column of her throat with his lips.

"Coming here was a mistake, Mor," he whispered. "You are surrounded by enemies. You know you won't survive the battle. I doubt even Galan could save you from the others' wrath if you fail."

"Then that is my fate." Her breathing caught as she answered. He felt her tremble under his touch. "I will not shrink from it."

Lust barreled into Talor then, setting his veins alight. He had never met anyone like this woman. She was a Serpent—Cathal mac Calum was her father. But right now none of that mattered. Mor had a dignity that he had never seen in anyone. Her quest for peace was futile, but he respected her for it. It was more worthy than his crazed lust for vengeance. Mor could see beyond the hate, beyond the need for reckoning—and she would gladly die for it.

With a sharply indrawn breath, Talor caught her chin and drew it lower so that their gazes fused for an instant. And then his mouth crashed down upon hers.

Chapter Eighteen

Poor Timing

THE KISS WAS brutal, searing. With Mor trapped between the cradle of his hands, Talor ravaged her mouth. He had not planned on kissing her, had not thought this through at all. Desire drove Talor now, pulsing through him like a battle drum. And his shaft turned rock hard when she responded to his embrace with equal ferocity.

Mor's lips parted under his, allowing his tongue to dive deep. Their lips crushed, and their teeth clashed; the kiss was hot and wild. And yet their bodies still did not touch—except for where Talor's fingers splayed across the back of Mor's skull, holding her firm in his embrace.

A heartbeat later the sound of someone clearing their throat interrupted them.

Breathing hard, Talor tore his mouth from Mor's and twisted his attention toward the entrance of the tent.

His uncle Galan stood there, his gaze narrowed, arms folded across his chest. "I think that's enough for now, Talor," he said gently. "It's time to go."

Talor glowered at his uncle. He had not given them any time at all alone. It seemed as if only a few moments had passed since the other chieftains left the tent. And yet there Galan was, looking at Talor as if he had just betrayed them all.

Talor released Mor, stepping back from her and dropping his hands. He felt the softness of her hair brush against his fingers as he did so.

And all the while, Mor did not speak. She merely watched him, her eyes luminous and her lips swollen from his kisses.

The Reaper take Galan—his uncle had poor timing.

Mor watched Talor stride from the tent without another word, brushing past the Eagle chieftain on the way out. Galan of The Eagle cast her a hard, lingering look, before he followed.

She wondered if Galan mac Muin believed she had tried to seduce his nephew—that she had lured Talor close with the intention of getting him to free her wrists from their bonds.

But truthfully, escape had been the last thing on her mind.

Alone in the tent, Mor let out a long trembling breath. What had just happened?

Her lips still stung from the kiss. She could still taste him, could still smell the musk of his skin. Hunger reared up within her. She could drown in the taste of him. And she longed for another kiss, for him to tangle his fingers in her hair and hold her fast as he savaged her mouth.

Mor's eyes fluttered shut. Lust was a distraction, and yet she welcomed it. This close to death, her senses were sharpened. The moment Talor had walked into the tent, the moment they had locked eyes, she had not cared what her fate would be. Her entire body tingled at the sight of him, and heat settled in the cradle of her hips.

He had cast an enchantment over her, and now she knew
that until she drew her last breath—and that moment
was coming soon—she would long for that arrogant man.

When he had kissed her, she felt a sense of
completeness that had eluded Mor her entire life. It was
like they were two broken pieces of the same amulet.
And when they came together, nothing else in this world
mattered.

Enough. She could not let her thoughts travel in such
a direction. Longing for something she could not have
made sadness compress her chest. Life could be
inordinately cruel at times. But to give her a glimpse of
what she wanted, and then hold it out of arms reach,
made Mor wonder what she had ever done to anger the
Gods so.

She sank down onto a pile of furs a few feet away
from the brazier. It was awkward, with her wrists bound
tightly behind her, but she managed to get comfortable,
propped up on her side, facing the entrance to the tent.
The flap hung closed, yet she knew there would be
warriors standing guard out there.

Mor frowned. She felt naked without her weapons,
the numerous blades she always kept strapped to her
body. Many warriors within this encampment had a
score to settle with The Serpent. They would want to do
her harm—and now was their chance. Of course, guards
ringed the tent, but how many of them also sought
vengeance against her people. She would not sleep easily
tonight.

Talor strode from the tent, intent on getting away
from his uncle as quickly as possible. However, it was
not to be.

"Talor." Galan's voice boomed out behind him. "A
moment, please."

Heaving a sigh, Talor turned, his boots crunching in
the snow. Around them the last of the day had faded, and
a chill night had settled over the world. The sky was
clear; a slender crescent moon rode high overhead. It

cast a hoary light over the sea of tents around the two men as they faced each other.

"I'm tired, uncle," Talor said. "Can this wait?"

Galan raised an eyebrow, folding his arms across his broad chest. It was a gesture that Talor knew well; the chieftain wanted answers.

"I see there is more to the tale you have both spun," Galan said. His voice was low and hard. He did not like being lied to.

Talor shook his head. "We both spoke the truth."

"But you left out an important detail. This woman is now your lover."

"She isn't," Talor countered, his brow furrowing. An ache rose under his ribs as he realized just how much he wished that was the case. As much as he wanted Mor, he could not have her now. "It was just a kiss."

Galan scowled, his grey eyes darkening. "There are many different types of kiss," he said, his voice developing a warning edge. "But that was not a casual one."

Talor stared back at him, not understanding what his uncle was insinuating.

After a beat, Galan's mouth unexpectedly quirked. "I was wondering when you'd finally fall for a lass."

Talor huffed a laugh, even if his gut twisted. "That's ridiculous." He raked a hand through his short hair, silently pleading for this conversation to end. "It was just a kiss ... can we leave it at that?"

"That's quite a collection of bruises you've got there." Eithni's voice was lightly chiding. "But they'll fade ... eventually."

Talor grunted. He sat on a low stool before the fire pit in his parents' tent. Stripped to the waist, he hunched over while his stepmother checked his bruises and grazes, and then rubbed ointment onto them. A few feet away, his little sister, Eara, watched him with wide eyes. Behind her, sitting cross-legged upon a fur as he sharpened a knife blade upon a whet-stone, Donnel looked on. The rhythmic scrape of iron against stone joined the gentle crackle of the fire.

"It could have been worse," Talor admitted. "I'm aware of that."

"Just as well that you are," Donnel spoke up. There was a flat edge to his voice that warned Talor his father was still smoldering. "The Gods were looking down on you it seems."

"I'm so happy you're back, Talor." Eara shuffled across to him, her small hands clasping his knee. "Everyone said you wouldn't return, but I knew you would. There is no one stronger or braver than you."

Talor's mouth twisted. Reaching out, he clasped his half-sister's small hands in his, squeezing gently. "I'm strong, but even I am mortal, little bird," he murmured. "I did a foolish thing. Make sure when you grow up, you think before you act."

"Wise words indeed, son." Donnel halted sharpening his blade. His voice had softened slightly. Talor realized that his contrition had unbalanced his father a little. It was not feigned; Talor was sorry for doing what he had done. But he could see his altered manner concerned Donnel.

"Not so wise," Talor said, glancing up and meeting his father's eye. "The words come from bitter experience."

"So, you no longer seek reckoning for Bonnie?" Donnel asked.

Talor considered the question. The anger was still there—a dark stain across his soul. But his fury had drawn back slightly. It no longer drove him as it had. "The Serpent must fall. We have to get Dun Ringill back," he replied after a pause. "But even if I am the one to sink a blade in Cathal mac Calum's belly, it will never return Bonnie to us."

Silence fell in the tent. After a spell, Eithni sat back on her heels and reached for a cloth to clean her hands. "We all miss Bonnie too, you know," she murmured. "Not a day goes by when I don't catch myself thinking about that lass—missing her laugh, the wicked glint in her eyes."

Talor turned and met his step-mother's gaze, his throat thickening. "I realize that now," he replied. "I entered a strange world after Bonnie died. It was like the rest of you were cut off from me. But I don't feel that way anymore.

"Have the past days altered you that much?" Donnel asked. Glancing his father's way, Talor saw he was observing him, his brow furrowed. His father was still perplexed by the change he saw in his son.

Talor's mouth lifted at the edges. "They have."

Chapter Nineteen
Moving Out

TALOR WAS IN an introspective mood when he left his parents' tent and stepped out into the gelid night. He felt the need to be alone for a little while. With a heavy fur mantle about his shoulders, he made his way through the encampment.

Sending away a warrior who had been taking his turn at the watch, Talor took his place at the perimeter. He then swept his gaze over the hill before him. The moonlight illuminated the snowy landscape in silver. He was gazing west. Just a few furlongs away in that direction rose the stone bulk of Dun Ringill.

Cathal would know that their army was waiting here. He would be preparing for the siege. It was a battle he could not win. Would he listen to his daughter and her words of reason?

Talor was not sure he would. He had spent little time in Cathal's company but had noted that he was a proud, stubborn man. And coming from a long line of bull-headed men, he recognized the type. The Serpent chieftain was not a warrior who easily backed down from a fight.

"There you are," a familiar voice sounded behind him.

Talor turned to see a tall, broad-shouldered figure approach. Muin, his cousin. He was leading a sturdy dappled grey pony.

Talor's face split into a grin at the sight of both of them. "What's Luath doing here?" He stepped forward and ran a hand down the pony's furry neck, wincing as the stallion nudged his bruised flank in greeting.

"We found the beast trampling vegetables in the fields outside Balintur," Muin replied. "I brought Luath with us ... for when we found you." The cousins' gazes met and held. "I never gave up hope we would."

Talor's grin faded. The pair of them were as close as brothers, and yet Talor had barely spoken to Muin since his return to the camp. In truth, he had been avoiding him.

As if sensing his cousin's embarrassment, Muin smiled. "Where have you been? I checked the perimeter earlier, and you weren't here."

"Eithni wanted to fuss over me," Talor replied.

"She probably had reason." Muin ran a critical eye over him. "I saw the state of you when you arrived. "You look better now."

"It's amazing what a wash and clean clothes will do for a man." Talor knew he was being flippant, but he did not want Muin to see how uneasy he was tonight.

Yet his cousin was not a dull-witted man. Muin's grey eyes narrowed, his jaw firming. "We really did think we'd seen the last of you," he said, his tone roughening. "Your parents were desperate."

Talor swallowed. "I know."

Muin continued to study him, in that intense way of his. Talor had never been able to hide much from him. He suddenly had the urge to tell his cousin about Mor, yet the words stuck in his throat. Muin would not judge him—but since Talor was still confused about the situation himself, he was not sure he wanted to open a discussion about it. As such, he held his tongue.

"Don't worry." Muin stepped forward and clapped him on the shoulder. "I'm not going to chew your ear off … I imagine your father's already done so."

Talor forced another smile. "Aye … why do you think I'm hiding out here?"

Mor awoke to a burning ache in her shoulders. She had fallen asleep with her arms twisted behind her. Stifling a groan, she pushed herself up and wiggled her fingers. Fortunately, her captors had not bound her wrists too tightly. Although they tingled a little, her hands had not gone numb.

A few feet away, the brazier burned low. The air inside the tent had turned chill, and watery light filtered in through the gaps in the roof. Dawn had come, and a meeting with her father awaited.

Mor's bowels cramped at the thought. Although she had put on a brave face, she dreaded going before her people. They would all think her a traitor. They would not understand.

Clenching her eyes shut, Mor reminded herself that she did not need everyone to understand—only her father had to.

She had to find a way to convince him.

Climbing to her feet, she was just stretching out the kinks in her back and legs when the tent flap drew aside and a woman ducked inside.

Disappointment stabbed Mor, as she realized she had hoped to see Talor. Last night's kiss, and the brief words they had shared, still lingered.

However, there was something familiar about the woman before her. Small and dark-haired, her lithe limbs smeared with woad, the warrior halted just inside the entrance and studied Mor for a long moment. Likewise, Mor stared back.

Despite the snowy weather, she dressed lightly, as many warrior women of this isle did. The fur wrapped around her shoulders was her only concession to the biting cold. A quiver of arrows and a longbow hung over one shoulder, and Mor noted that she had numerous blades strapped to her body.

"I'm Fina," the woman said after a lengthy pause. "Talor's cousin."

A slight smile lifted the corners of Mor's mouth as she continued to hold the newcomer's gaze. Of course. Talor came from a line of warriors. She could feel the same restless energy emanating from Fina that Talor often displayed.

She nodded a wary greeting to Fina. It was hard to tell whether this woman was as hostile to her as many of the others had been, for she wore an impassive expression. Her grey eyes were hard and watchful—the same storm-grey as The Eagle chieftain's.

"Is it time, then?" Mor asked.

"Aye ... I'm to take you out so you can visit the privy, and then we shall join the others."

Mor nodded, before she moved toward Fina. As she drew closer, she realized that she towered over the woman. The females of this isle were much smaller than she was used to, although even among her own people, Mor was taller than most other women. Fina made her feel like a giantess. But the warrior did not appear intimidated by her height in the least. She merely stepped back, motioning for Mor to leave the tent ahead of her.

Outdoors, a grey morning greeted Mor. The air was damp, and the bone-numbing cold drilled into her flesh, easily penetrating the layers of clothing she wore. Without her cloak, she felt the chill keenly.

The sky had a faint pinkish tinge to it, a sign that the brief spell of clear skies was coming to an end. More snow was on its way.

Fina led Mor through the encampment, to an area that had been fenced off behind a makeshift perimeter of hide: a privy of sorts. The warrior was not on her own though. A group of warriors—those who had guarded Mor's tent during the night—followed close behind, just in case Mor tried anything.

A bitter smile curved Mor's mouth as she cast a glance over her shoulder at them. Did they really think she would try to escape after she had given herself up voluntarily?

Fina followed her behind the hide screen and deftly unbound her wrists so that Mor could relieve herself. Squatting in the snow, Mor sighed as she emptied her tight bladder. She then rose to her feet and relaced her plaid leggings. "I'm ready to go."

Fina nodded, her expression remaining neutral. She then moved behind Mor and rebound her wrists. "There are some oatcakes left ... do you want any?"

Mor shook her head. The prospect of facing her father this morning had closed her stomach. She was not hungry in the slightest. However, she was thirsty. "Just some ale will do," she replied.

Fina led her out from behind the screens, and they trudged through the snow to the western side of the encampment. Despite that dawn was fully upon them now, there was no sign of anyone packing up to leave. Mor realized then that this camp would remain during the siege. The army of the warriors of the united tribes had settled in. They were not planning on going anywhere until Dun Ringill fell.

Hostile gazes followed Mor's path through the camp.

A woman bearing the mark of The Stag upon her right bicep spat at Mor when she walked past. "Serpent turd."

Mor ignored the insult and the others that followed. Fina walked at her side, not paying the hisses and mutters any mind. The hatred Mor saw in their eyes did not surprise her in the least. This was why she had come here, why she had broken with her own people.

Hatred like this could only end in bloodshed for them all. And it would not end with this siege; it would just dig its roots deep into this land and poison it for generations. Mor had witnessed this happen upon the mainland. She did not want the same thing to happen here. The chieftains of the united tribes were vehemently against sharing this isle with her tribe, but she still had not given up hope.

The first step would be getting her father to listen.

Approaching the western edge of the camp, she spied the army waiting for her. Mor stopped next to Fina, her gaze sweeping the ranks of men and women who awaited orders to move out. She breathed in the restless, nervous energy that vibrated through the crowd—as it always did before battle. She witnessed the steely looks upon the warrior's faces, their hard gazes.

Mor's chest tightened at the sight of them; their numbers were huge, far greater than she had anticipated. Her father could never hold Dun Ringill for long if he were to face such a horde.

"Fina ... there you are!"

A strange woman strode toward them. Mor knew at a glance that she was a bandruí, for her long dark hair was braided in many tiny plaits, her shapely limbs rattling with bone jewelry.

Murdina might have looked like her once, Mor thought. However, this woman, who carried a pot of burning herbs and a slender divining rod, was much taller than their elderly seer. And as she drew near, Mor saw that the woman was beautiful—with startling sea-blue eyes of a familiar hue.

"Is she a relation to Talor?" Mor asked Fina.

The warrior raised her eyebrows, surprised that Mor had broken the silence between them with such a question. She handed Mor a bladder of ale before answering. "Aye, they are cousins ... they both lost their mothers young."

Fina had just finished speaking when the seer stopped before them. She murmured words in a low, musical voice, the divining wand moving over them both.

Mor stiffened. "Why are you blessing me?" she asked, her tone sharper than she had intended. "I'm one of the enemy."

The bandruí's gaze met hers, holding her fast. "You came to us seeking peace," she said, her tone low and firm. "I do not see you as my foe."

Fina snorted at this. "Careful, Ailene ... don't let anyone overhear you saying that."

The seer's gaze narrowed. "Maybe they should listen to me," she replied. "I cast the bones again this morning, and they tell me the same as they did upon the Long Night ... there will be a union between The Eagle and The Serpent."

Mor's breathing hitched at these words. She stared at Ailene. "Talor and I visited our bandruí a couple of days ago," she began softly. "And she told us something similar."

Ailene's pretty features tightened. "What did she say?"

Mor hesitated then. She had deliberately avoided bringing up the subject, for she knew it would not be well-received. The likes of Wid of The Wolf had been itching to call her a liar. And judging from the fierce look upon Fina's face, the seer was the only one receptive to the news. "She was vague," Mor mumbled, tearing her gaze from Ailene's and focusing on the hills to the west, "but she said something about the future lying in an alliance between our peoples."

Fina was frowning now. "Talor hasn't mentioned visiting your seer. Why didn't you say anything about this before?"

Mor shrugged, her attention swiveling back to the warrior woman. "I don't know why Talor didn't speak of this ... but I didn't think any of you would believe such a tale. I imagined you would think I was trying to manipulate you."

Fina's jaw tightened. "And aren't you?"

"No." The word was hard and flat, and a tense silence followed in its wake.

A few yards away, Mor spotted Talor then. Rested and clothed in fresh leathers, a fur cloak hanging from his shoulders, he strode through the crowd toward her. A tall, broad-shouldered warrior with long dark hair, grey eyes, and a stern expression followed him.

Reaching the women, Talor stopped. His gaze swept over them, taking in the strained looks upon their faces.

"We're moving out now," he informed them, before his gaze met Mor's.

For a long moment their gazes held. Heat rushed through Mor as she remembered their kiss the night before.

She had been surprised at his boldness, at how he had moved close and taken hold of her before running his lips in a sensual caress down the column of her throat. He had no idea how that had excited her. Her entire body had pulsed with need, even before he had claimed her mouth with his.

That same aching want pulsed through her now, making her forget why she was standing here, and what lay ahead.

Talor's next words shattered the illusion.

"Ready to face your father?"

Mor grimaced. "No ... but I will all the same."

Chapter Twenty

No Daughter of Mine

THE SIGHT OF Dun Ringill before her made Mor's heart start to pound. It was strange really. She was never this nervous before battle; she had grown up readying herself to fight.

But this meeting was different. This time she was to go before her father and look him in the eye as she spoke of peace.

Her dread increased with every step.

She walked ahead of where the four chieftains of the united tribes rode upon shaggy ponies. Her wrists were still bound behind her, and Galan had leashed her to him with a long chain lest she try to run off.

The walls of the fort looked dull and cold, outlined against a flat grey sky. Despite that a new day had dawned, braziers still glowed atop the walls. Mor scanned the defenses, noting the spears that thrust up against the heavens. They would likely have barrels of burning pitch up there, ready to tip down upon the attackers. She wondered whether she should warn the chieftains about that—but then decided she would hold her tongue.

Her mission this morning was to convince all of them to lay down their weapons. She would not focus on anything else.

The army drew to a halt, a furlong back from the outer walls, and waited for Cathal to come to them. This was how a siege always began, with talks beforehand. More often than not this conversation was not a peace negotiation but rather an exchange of insults, of boasts, designed to rile their opponents all the more so that they went into battle baying for each other's blood.

Mor continued to study the fort, her keen gaze scrutinizing every detail. The outer walls were undefended. Her people had pulled back from the village and barricaded themselves inside the inner perimeter. That was wise, for the outer walls would be impossible to hold for long, and the gates into the village were flimsy compared to the great iron and wooden slabs that prevented access to the broch itself.

Mor was not surprised her father had pulled back. Even so, the sight of the open gate made her already racing heart leap. At first glance it looked as if Cathal was going to just hand over the fort to his enemy. However, she knew he would not.

Three ponies emerged from the outer gate.

Cathal mac Calum approached them now, riding ahead upon a feather-footed bay stallion—a horse that he had stolen from Tarl mac Muin the previous summer. Mor had spotted Tarl riding behind the four chieftains. She recognized the warrior instantly, for he had been their captive for a few months earlier. This morning she had also discovered that Tarl was Fina's father—a fact that had not surprised her. The eyes gave her away.

Behind Tarl rode Talor and his own father, Donnel mac Muin. Tall, proud, and dark-haired, father and son looked uncannily alike. Donnel had not spoken to Mor before they rode out from camp. Instead, his stormy gaze had fixed upon her, unflinching and hostile.

Although she knew that Talor and his father would still be watching her now, Mor was not concentrating on the ranks of warriors behind her, or the glares that bored a hole in her back. Instead, her attention was riveted on the tall, muscular warrior with wild auburn hair who pulled up his pony a few yards away. Two warriors drew up their ponies behind him; one of them was Tormud. The Boar warrior's hard gaze swept over the lines of warriors before him, his eyes smoldering with hate when they settled upon Mor.

Mor ignored him. Her attention never wavered from her father.

Cathal's gaze was riveted upon her, his lantern jaw rigid. For a heartbeat Mor realized that he was worried for her. For just an instant, she allowed him to believe that Talor had escaped without her help and had taken her prisoner. In this frozen moment in time, she had not betrayed his trust and gone to the enemy to seek peace. He was just a concerned father, and she his only surviving child.

Mor's throat constricted, a familiar dull ache surfacing just under her breast bone. She did not want to disappoint him; she had lived her life wanting only to please her father. But now she stood upon the edge of a precipice. And once she jumped, there was no going back.

"You have something that belongs to me, I see," Cathal broke the silence, his voice cutting through the wind that whistled through the fort, blowing in from the sea.

"Mor is ours now, Serpent." Varar mac Urcal spoke up, his voice arrogant, deliberately provoking. "And I believe she has something to say to you."

Mor resisted the urge to cut The Boar chieftain a vicious look. She had not expected a long preamble before the moment when she would have to speak. But Varar had not wasted time in throwing her to the wolves.

Heaving in a deep breath, Mor met her father's eye. His gaze was flat, although she could see the worry that flickered there. He wanted to believe the best of her.

And she was now going to disappoint him.

"Da," she began, her voice husky. "I come before you to ask that we may have peace between our peoples."

Tension rippled over Cathal mac Calum's face. He did not speak, did not react. Instead, he waited for his daughter to explain herself.

"I freed our prisoner." She forced out the admission. It was so hard to say this to her father. He was the one person she feared disappointing. "And I gave myself up voluntarily to the warriors of the united tribes."

Something feral moved in the depths of her father's eyes. "And why would you do that, daughter?" he asked, his voice dangerously soft.

"Because I want an end to war," she replied, raising her chin to meet his stare head on. "All I have ever known is conflict and violence. You promised us all that a new life awaited us on this isle, yet the bloodshed has increased. I want you to stop this now." She paused there, heart hammering. "I have spoken with these chieftains ... they have agreed that if you lay down arms and surrender to them this morning, they will spare all your lives."

Mor stopped speaking, letting her words settle in. She knew from the thunderous look on Tormud's face, and the stony expression that settled over her father's features, that her plea was not well received.

She had not expected it would be—yet it was up to her to convince them.

Tormud spat on the ground, making his opinion evident.

"Traitorous bitch." Cathal's words lashed across Mor, and it took all her will not to flinch. "You are no daughter of mine."

"Father," Mor cut in, desperation rising within her. "It is your right to be angry with me, to cast me from your side. I deserve it for betraying your trust. But know this ... I didn't do it to hurt you. I am trying to save you ... to save our people."

Cathal's face twisted, and, straining his neck forward, he spat on the snow, mirroring Tormud's gesture.

Sensing its rider's fury, his stallion pawed the ground, its nostrils flaring. "You think surrender is going to help me?" he snarled. "You would have me crawl on all fours before these men ... you would have all honor stripped from me?"

"No," Mor choked out the denial. "I would have your lives spared. Why can't you see that? Why can't you understand?"

"Coward!"

That insult made Mor flinch, even if anger now curled up inside her, entwining with the desperation that clawed at her breast.

"I'd listen to your daughter if I were you." Galan mac Muin's low voice cut through the tension. "If it were up to us, you wouldn't be getting a second chance, Serpent. If your daughter had not pleaded on your behalf, there would be no negotiation at all. Our offer is a generous one, and far more than you deserve. Drop your weapons and surrender to us, and we will spare your lives."

"Shove your offer up your arse!" Cathal's roar echoed across the snowy clifftop. "I will not surrender. Instead, you will break against the walls of *my* broch like waves upon a shore. Do your worst. We will outlast you."

With that, Cathal reined his stallion around and kicked it into a stumbling canter through the snow. Tormud and his companion followed him back into the fort.

A heavy silence settled over the world then, and Mor's vision blurred. Her father had spoken. There would be no surrender—and so no chance of peace. The last shreds of hope fell away, and Mor's legs buckled under her. Her knees sank into the snow as she stared after her father, willing him to turn around, to change his mind.

But he did not. And as Mor watched him disappear, snow started to flutter down.

There would be no more negotiations between them now. Only death.

"Well, that was a waste of everyone's time," Wid of The Wolf muttered behind her. "I could have told you he wasn't going to back down."

"It was worth a try, Wid," Galan of The Eagle replied, a note of censure in his gruff voice. "Would you have gone against your own father like that?"

The question was met with silence. Mor did not look their way. Instead, she dropped her gaze to the snowy ground. Fresh flakes were now settling there. An icy wind bit into her, but she paid it no mind.

Coward.

Her father's insult had cut her deep, had ripped a piece of her heart away. She realized then how foolish she had been. She had truly believed he could be swayed, that his love for her would allow her to reach him.

But the opposite had happened. When she looked into her father's eyes, before he turned away, all she had seen was rage and burning hate. She was truly alone now. She wondered then, the thought rising sluggishly through the churning anguish, what would become of her.

Would they slay her here and now, or would they drag her into battle with them, to be offered up as a sacrifice—the ultimate insult to Cathal mac Calum.

Tears stung, and Mor squeezed her eyes shut, forcing them back. A warrior did not weep.

"On your feet lass." Galan tugged at the chain attached to her wrists. "It's time to go."

Mor struggled up, head hanging, and awaited the sentence. But when silence stretched out, she raised her chin to meet The Eagle chieftain's gaze. Galan was watching her, an enigmatic expression upon his hawkish face. The other three chieftains also observed her keenly.

Feeling another stare piercing her, Mor's attention shifted to the tall, dark-haired warrior who stood behind them. Talor watched her, his handsome face taut, his eyes shadowed. The moment drew out, and then Mor looked back to the men who would now decide her fate.

Galan shifted his attention to Varar. The two men's gazes fused for a heartbeat, and then Galan looked to Wid and Tadhg. "Does Mor deserve to die for her efforts?" he asked, his voice a low rumble. "Or shall we spare her for now?"

His gaze rested upon Wid, the chieftain who Mor sensed bore the greatest grudge against her people. No one had said as much, but she guessed that he had lost loved ones in this conflict.

Wid's heavy brow furrowed, his bearded face growing stern. He knew that Galan was putting the decision in his hands.

"Take the woman away," Wid muttered finally. "We can decide her fate once the siege is done."

Mor drew in a shaky breath, despair rather than relief settling over her. She had failed her people.

Glancing back at the walls of Dun Ringill, she then settled her attention on Galan once more. She was about to betray her father once more—but if the siege was going to take place, it was best that it did not drag out. "Be wary of the walls of the inner perimeter," she said after a pause. "We've been busy preparing pitch for any attack. They will have barrels of it burning up there ... and will be waiting for you to get underneath them."

Chapter Twenty-one

The Siege Begins

TALOR STUMBLED BACK, raising his shield as a stream of bubbling black liquid cascaded down from the top of the wall. As Mor had warned, The Serpent were attempting to douse them with burning pitch.

The acrid odor stung the back of Talor's throat while he scanned the surging crowd of warriors gathered at the base of the wall; like him, they had been wary of approaching.

The Cruthini were clearly efficient at making pitch—a black tarry substance created from melted pine resin. Dun Ringill already had a few barrels of it, although they had obviously been busy making more over the past months.

Mor had saved a number of lives in warning them about it.

"Keep your distance," he shouted to the other warriors. "They'll run out of pitch eventually ... and when they do, we'll put up ladders."

After issuing the order, Talor shifted farther back from the wall, lowered his shield, and joined the line of archers who were picking off as many Cruthini as they could from the top of the high perimeter that encircled the broch. Talor unslung his own bow, drew an arrow from the quiver upon his back, and notched it. His mouth thinned as he scanned the top of the wall, looking for a target.

His forefathers had done a good job when they built Dun Ringill. They had constructed this wall over twenty feet high and four feet thick. He remembered how exhausting the climb had been when he had scaled its seaward side.

His grandfather had added further defenses to the inner perimeter during his time as chieftain: high stone crenellations that gave those defending the top of the wall, and archers, something to hide behind.

But The Serpent could not cower there forever. Sooner or later, they would have to emerge from the stone defenses, and when they did, he would be ready.

A bulky figure clad in leather and fur appeared then, ducking out from behind the stone wall.

Talor's arrow hissed as it flew from his bow. It found its mark, striking the warrior in the chest. With a strangled cry, arms wheeling, the man fell to his death.

"Good shot," Fina grunted from beside him. She then loosed an arrow that narrowly missed a Cruthini's skull as he poked his head over the crenellation. She muttered a curse. "Almost had him."

"Patience," Talor counseled her. Although Fina was skilled with a bow, he had always been the better of the two of them. He was not a patient man by nature, but when it came to getting the right shot with his bow, he could wait for an eternity. Not so, Fina.

"This is ridiculous," she growled. "Let me draw my sword and fight with the others at the wall."

"And defy your husband's wishes?" Talor did not take his gaze off the top of the defenses as he replied. The enemy had just emptied another barrel of flaming pitch over the side, causing the tide of attackers to draw back even farther. "Varar's only trying to take care of you."

"I should have known you would take his side," Fina muttered. She loosed another arrow then, and this time it found its mark, piercing a Cruthini through the leg. The man, who had foolishly ventured out into the open for a moment, collapsed on the wall, disappearing from sight.

"Aye, you are carrying a bairn, Fina," Talor countered as he drew another arrow and notched it. "If it were up to me, you wouldn't be taking part in this siege at all … but Varar knows we need your skill with a bow. However, if I catch you sneaking up to the front, I'll drag you back by the hair myself."

"Just you try," Fina replied. Talor allowed himself a grim smile. Even without looking her way, he knew his cousin would be glaring at him ferociously. It mattered not. He stood firmly with Varar on this. Fina was not to put herself and the bairn she carried at risk.

Focusing once more on the wall, he narrowed his gaze. Around him the snow gusted in, swirling thickly. If it snowed any heavier, it would impede the archers' visibility. The siege was going slower than he would have liked. The snow shrouded their vision, and as Mor had warned, the enemy had numerous barrels of burning pitch. While they lasted, they could not risk climbing the wall or getting a battering ram near the gates.

Talor's jaw tightened then. Sooner or later the pitch would run out—and when it did, they would be ready.

Night was settling over the ivory-colored hills when the army drew back from Dun Ringill and returned to the encampment. Standing on the edge, her hands still bound behind her back, Mor watched them arrive.

Their numbers seemed as great as they had been that morning—so her father's warriors had not managed to weaken them—although many of the approaching men and women were scowling.

At a glance she realized that the siege was progressing slowly.

Of course it will, she reminded herself, and despite everything, pride surged. *My father defends Dun Ringill.*

Cathal mac Calum was a veteran of many sieges. He knew how to hold out against the enemy; only, she was aware how limited their supplies were inside the broch, and how few warriors there were to defend it. Once the attackers started putting up ladders, it would be hard to stem the tide; and once they breached the gates, it would be over for those inside.

Her belly twisted at the thought, cold sweat beading upon her skin.

The despair that had consumed her at dawn sloughed away, her stubborn will surfacing once more.

I won't give up.

She had to make sure they did not slaughter everyone once they entered the broch. She had to try once more to get the chieftains of the united tribes to show mercy for her people.

Flanked by two warriors, Mor continued to watch the approaching army. They reached the outskirts of the camp, flowing past her. Many of them did not even spare her a glance, although one or two spat on the ground as they strode by.

Mor did not flinch, did not respond. She could hardly expect any better. Her fingers curled, her fingernails biting into her palms. It did not matter if she was an outcast; she would not lose hope.

She spotted Talor then. Relief swept through her; a welcome distraction from the isolation she felt. She was glad to see he still lived, for she had been worried he might do something reckless during the first day of the siege—something that might cost him his life.

Talor strode through the midst of the milling crowd toward her, his cousin Fina just a few feet behind him. Both of them had tired, pale faces, their expressions strained. The snow had continued to fall throughout the day, and Mor knew that would have made the siege even harder.

Fina cast Mor a baleful glance before continuing past her; however, Talor halted. Standing just a couple of feet apart, they looked at each other.

"How did it go?" Mor asked, her voice barely above a whisper.

"Slowly," Talor replied.

Studying him, Mor noted that although he looked exhausted and chilled to the marrow, the swelling on his face had now subsided greatly. His injuries were healing.

When she did not speak again, Talor's mouth lifted at the corners. "You were right about the burning pitch." He paused there. "But thanks to you, they wasted most of it."

Their gazes held, and suddenly Mor did not care that she stood amidst a sea of frustrated warriors who would gladly shove a blade through her guts.

At least there was no hostility in Talor's loch-blue eyes.

Eventually, Mor swallowed, breaking the spell. "I betrayed my people," she said huskily. "I want that to mean something."

He stepped closer still. "It already has, Mor."

Talor watched Mor walk away, flanked by two guards. They were leading her back to her tent, where she would continue to be guarded until the chieftains decided her fate.

It was not safe for her out here, not when everyone's blood was up. It had been a long, cold, and frustrating day—and there were likely to be more of them to come, before they managed to break through The Serpents' defenses. Nevertheless, Mor had already helped them significantly.

She walked tall and proud, her broad shoulders set, but Talor had seen the strain upon Mor's face. This morning had nearly broken her, and yet she was already rallying. He had seen the dogged determination in her eyes, before she turned away. Mor was far from beaten.

The woman was even stronger than he had realized. She was magnificent.

Tearing his gaze from Mor's retreating back, he clenched his hands by his sides. *What's happening to you?*

"Is something amiss, Talor?" The rumble of Muin's voice roused him. Talor glanced up to find two of his cousins standing before him: Muin and his younger brother, Aaron. Muin's brow was furrowed in concern, while Aaron wore a strained expression.

"Are your injuries paining you?" Muin asked.

Talor shook his head. The bruises, even those that had gone deep, were fading. "I'm fine," he said roughly. "Just ill-tempered."

Aaron snorted. "Just your usual self then?"

Talor raised an eyebrow and considered his young cousin a moment. Aaron had only recently reached manhood, and like Talor at the same age, he could be insufferably cocky—a freshly blooded warrior with something to prove. In the past, Aaron's quip would have been an invitation to bite back, but this evening Talor merely favored him with a tired smile.

He slung an arm around Aaron's shoulders, steering him toward the heart of the camp, where a great fire pit now burned. Wordlessly, Muin fell in behind the two of them. Talor cast a glance over his shoulder at him. "I think we've all earned ourselves a horn of mead and a hot meal, don't you think?"

Muin grunted his agreement. The aroma of boar stew reached them then, and Talor's mouth filled with saliva. Of course, while they had been trying to get close to the inner walks of Dun Ringill, the women who had accompanied them to the camp had been preparing a meal for when they returned.

A crowd of warriors now jostled around the fire, eager hands reaching for steaming bowls of stew. Muin, Aaron, and Talor joined them.

"There you all are!" A tall, dark-haired woman dressed in a long plaid skirt and a thick woolen tunic, a heavy cloak wrapped around her shoulders, approached them. Ailene's face stretched into a smile as she held out a tray containing three bowls of stew. "I kept these back for you."

Warmth spread through Talor at the sight of his cousin, although as soon as she had flashed him a smile, her attention shifted to Muin. Talor watched her drink him in. Ailene handed Talor and Aaron their bowls, before she went to Muin. He pulled her close, lowering his mouth to hers for a passionate kiss. "It's good to see you, mo ghràdh," he murmured.

Talor smiled at the affection between them. Muin and Ailene had been friends since childhood although for the past few years, Muin had carried a secret love for the comely seer. Unfortunately, Ailene had been blind to his passion for her, and determined to resist her own feelings, until a sequence of events a few months earlier had brought them together.

Muin and Ailene broke apart and gazed into each other's eyes. Watching them, Talor suddenly felt like an intruder. He picked up the wooden spoon in the stew and took a large mouthful, moving away from the couple toward where Aaron was already devouring his supper. The food was hot, scalding his tongue, yet he was too hungry to care.

But even the hot stew could not fill the gnawing emptiness that now clawed at his gut.

Chapter Twenty-two
With My Help

STANDING BEFORE THE brazier in her tent, huddling as close as she dared to its heat, Mor went over the plan she had been mulling over for the past couple of days. It was risky—and was likely to spell her own doom—but she could see no other way forward.

The siege of Dun Ringill had lasted three days so far.

The defenders still held the fort. The snow had fallen steadily since the attack had begun. It had made visibility difficult and worked in her father's favor.

The assault of burning pitch had ceased, but instead, Cruthini archers sent down a hail of arrows from the top of wall.

By the end of the third day of the siege, the attackers were in a fury. They returned to Dun Ringill in a foul mood. Sensing tension in the air, Mor remained within her tent as dusk settled. She heard the rough voices and felt the tension that filled the camp with the return of the army.

It was best to let them calm down a little, before she showed her face.

Heaving a sigh, Mor stretched out her chilled fingers over the glowing lump of peat. This conflict was taking its toll on her now; her nerves felt stretched taut. She had awoken with a stiff jaw that morning, after clenching it in her sleep.

At the end of the first day of battle, the chieftains had questioned her further about her father's defenses. Mor had answered them, yet each answer she had given had been like a knife wound to her heart. Each new betrayal cut her deeper.

But it had been necessary. She needed to gain these men's trust.

Her father's reaction to her plea still haunted her. She had hoped that he would listen to her, and still tasted the bitterness of disappointment in the aftermath. But there had to be another way. Her failure on the first day had only made her more determined.

Mor was a fighter; she would not give up. She had to do something to ensure she was present when Dun Ringill finally fell. She needed to be able to plead for her people one last time.

Flexing her fingers, Mor's eyelids fluttered shut for a few moments. A familiar hollow sensation settled in her belly. She had felt so alone over the past days. She had hoped Talor would visit her again, but there had been no sign of him since the evening of the first day of the siege. She wondered if he deliberately stayed away.

Squeezing her eyes shut, she finally made her decision.

She dreaded what she must do, for it would require further sacrifice from her. She would need to sever herself entirely from her tribe in order to save them—but it was either that or allow every last one of them to be slaughtered. Aye, for the moment they were holding Dun Ringill, but their defenses were close to breaking. She knew it.

The thought of her people's destruction suddenly made it hard to breathe. Mor lifted her chin, her eyes snapping open.

It's time.

Moving away from the brazier, Mor pushed her way, head first, through the flap that covered the entrance to the tent. There, two big men bearing ash spears barred her way.

One of them raised an eyebrow, fixing her with a gimlet stare. "Going somewhere?"

Mor stared back at him, her jaw tensing. "I need to speak to the chieftains. Take me to them."

Talor pulled the collar of his fur mantle up, in an attempt to protect the back of his neck from the wind's teeth. That was the problem with cutting his hair short. The warriors with long hair had more protection from the cold. Like his father, Talor preferred to shear his dark-hair close to his scalp. He did not like to give the enemy anything to grab onto in battle.

Night had fallen, and the chill that settled over the encampment was numbing; it felt the worst of the bitter season so far.

"The Reaper's cods," Muin muttered beside him. "It's cold enough to freeze off your balls."

Talor managed a grimace of a smile. "At least it's stopped snowing."

Muin gave a terse nod, his gaze shifting back to where the four chieftains stood around the fire pit before them. Although Talor and Muin did not take part in discussions, they joined the chieftains each night as they talked over the day's progress and made a plan for the following day.

Listening to them, Talor felt excitement kindle in his belly. The past few days had been frustrating, but they had known taking back Dun Ringill would not be easy. He noted that the chieftains were deferring to Galan. No one knew the broch's defenses like he did; they would expect him to lead the way into the fort.

And Talor would be right up at the front—at his uncle's side.

"If you let me fight alongside you, I will reveal how my father will defend the broch once the gates are breached."

A cool female voice interrupted them then—and all gazes swiveled to where a tall woman, with wild auburn hair, shouldered her way through the crowd.

Talor's breathing hitched. Even with her wrists bound behind her, and shadowed by two hulking warriors, Mor was striking. If she felt any fear at standing before the chieftains, at being surrounded by men and women who had bayed for her blood through the campaign so far, she did not show it.

Instead, Mor was watching Galan. "My father's not defeated yet," she said, her voice steady, betraying no emotion at all. Likewise, her moss-green eyes were shuttered. "But I can help you bring him down faster."

Galan shared a look with Varar beside him, before he finally answered. "And how can we do that?" he asked.

Talor heard the suspicion in his uncle's voice and did not blame him. His own gaze narrowed as he stared at Mor, willing her to look his way. But she did not. *What is she up to?*

"Free me ... allow me to remain on this isle ... and let me fight alongside you tomorrow, and I will tell you everything I know," she replied.

These words caused surprise to ripple through the surrounding crowd. Talor shared a glance with Muin. His cousin was scowling, while next to him, Ailene was watching Mor intently. A few feet away, standing next to Varar, Fina was glaring at Mor, suspicion bright in her eyes.

Talor shifted his attention back to Mor, hoping to catch her eye. But still she did not look his way. Instead, she continued to watch Galan, her gaze unwavering. To look at her you would think she was made of stone. And yet Talor remembered how he had managed to ignite her temper back at that hunter's hut, and how she had responded to his kiss the night before the siege had begun. Underneath that ice shield, this woman was pure fire.

But she kept that part of herself carefully hidden as she faced the chieftains.

"Why would you want to fight alongside us?" Galan asked Mor, frowning.

"I gave my father a chance to surrender," she replied, her voice lowering. Her gaze shadowed then. "But he refused ... and disowned me ... I owe him nothing. It's time to look to my own future. When Dun Ringill falls, I want to be a free woman. This isle has become home to me. I want to stay here."

Listening to these words, Talor tensed. He had never seen this side to Mor before. He had not realized she could be so pragmatic, so cold-blooded.

Galan turned to the other chieftains. "Do we trust her?"

Wid's face screwed up. "We can't trust a Serpent."

"And yet the woman has not betrayed us as yet," Varar reminded him quietly. "She did try to convince her father to surrender. She also told us about the burning pitch ... and if she hadn't many of our warriors would have been maimed or killed. Everything we have asked of her, she has given."

The Boar chieftain's words surprised Talor. As always, you could never read Varar's expression. He kept his shield up, especially during meetings like these. And yet his words contrasted with his expression.

"She is willing to betray her own father," Tadhg answered, scowling. "If she can do that ... she would turn on us in a heartbeat."

"Betraying my father is the hardest thing I have ever done." Mor's voice cut through their midst, the tremble in it revealing the war she was fighting within. "It rips out my heart ... but there comes a time when we all must decide what's worth living and dying for." Her eyes burned now, huge against the paleness of her face.

"And your freedom is more important to you than kin?" Wid growled, his lip curling as he met Mor's eye.

Mor's face went rigid. "I did my best to work for peace, to save my people from this fate ... but I won't sacrifice myself for a man who no longer recognizes me as his daughter."

Wid barked a laugh at this, although there was no mirth in it. No one around the fire joined him.

"It's a lonely path you've chosen, lass." Galan spoke up once more. However, his gaze was not angry, but concerned. "Even if you earn your freedom and remain upon this isle, you'll still be an outcast."

Mor's throat bobbed, and she held Galan's gaze for a long moment, before she answered. "Let me worry about that," she whispered. "I know how my father thinks ... how he will defend the broch tomorrow. Don't under-estimate him. He's more dangerous than ever when cornered."

Chapter Twenty-three

Bravery Turns into Madness

A HEAVY SILENCE followed Mor's words.

There was no muttering this time, just uneasy looks and a tension in the air that you could have cut with a knife.

Talor's belly clenched. He did not know what Mor was doing, but this recklessness he now witnessed in her concerned him. She had the eyes of a doomed warrior, the same light he was sure his own gaze held when he had ridden to Dun Ringill on his quest to kill Cathal mac Calum.

Mor was not going to let this go.

She wanted her freedom—no matter what it cost her.

"I don't know whether you are ruthless, brave, or goose-witted, lass," Tadhg's low voice broke the silence. "But if you wish to fight at our side tomorrow, to help us bring your father down, then I agree to setting you free, to letting you live out the remainder of your days upon The Winged Isle."

The Stag chieftain shifted his gaze between the three remaining chieftains. "What about the rest of you?"

"I agree," Galan answered. However, Talor noted the wariness in his uncle's gaze. Like Talor, this whole scene was making him uncomfortable.

"I too agree," Varar added.

"So that just leaves me ... again." Wid folded brawny arms across his chest. "Why does the last word always rest with The Wolf?"

"Take it as a compliment," Varar replied with a snort. "What will it be, Wid?"

The Wolf chieftain huffed out a long sigh, before he fixed Mor with a dark look. "I don't understand you, lass. But if you are set on taking this betrayal of yours to its limit then, aye ... fight with us tomorrow."

Mor swallowed, before she nodded.

Galan turned to one of the men flanking Mor. "Free her."

The warrior did as bid, stepping behind Mor and untying the cord that bound her wrists. Unspeaking, Mor shook out her hands, her face tensing as blood rushed back into her fingers. Then, rubbing the red welts upon her wrists where the cord had bit in, she met Galan's eye once more.

"Are you ready to hear this?"

"Aye," Galan replied. "Tell us everything."

The bairn came into the world wailing. The babe's cries shook the broch, echoing high into the smoke-blackened rafters.

"He's a fighter, this one," Cathal told the tired mother as she leaned back against a nest of furs, her eyes hollowed with exhaustion and shadowed with grief. The lad still bawled as he lay against her breast. "He'll not go easily to The Reaper."

The woman, Edina, favored him with a wan smile. "Then I shall name him 'Bhaltair'," she murmured. "He who is as strong as a bear."

Cathal, who stood at the entrance to the alcove where Edina had given birth, managed a smile in return, even if a strange sensation had now gripped his ribs in a vise. "A fine choice of name."

His gaze shifted then to the healer, Lessa. She was the tall, heavy-set woman who was tending to Edina, readying her to pass the afterbirth. It was time to leave them. Apart from the healer, Edina had given birth on her own. Her man had not been present to stroke her back or hold her hand.

Gill had fallen the day before, on the walls, and the shock had sent Edina into labor.

Feeling as if he had a boulder sitting in his belly, Cathal let the curtain drop and walked to the far end of the feasting hall. There, he stepped up onto the raised platform and took his seat at the chieftain's table. Supper had ended, and only two others sat there: Artair and Tormud.

The former caught Cathal's eye when he sat down, while the latter helped himself to another horn of mead.

"The bairn was not due for nearly another moon ... is it well?" Artair asked.

Cathal nodded. "Lessa tells me that the birth wasn't an overly difficult one ... the bairn is small but healthy, as is his mother."

"Not that it will do either of them any good," Artair replied, a rasp to his voice. "The enemy won't care that the bairn is newborn ... they'll slay him like everyone else in this broch."

"All the more reason to defend the fort well tomorrow then," Tormud quipped from a few feet away. "I tire of your whining, Artair ... you've turned into a woman of late."

Ignoring the jibe, Artair held his brother's gaze. "The gates won't hold much longer, will they?"

Cathal clenched his jaw. He wanted to argue with his brother, to deny the question, and yet suddenly he felt too weary to do so. After a long silence, he shook his head.

Artair cut Tormud a look of simmering resentment, before he focused once more on his brother. "When they break through, it won't matter how well we defend the fort. They outnumber us vastly now. Their sheer numbers will overwhelm us. You know this, brother. Look me in the eye, and deny I'm telling the truth."

The brothers stared at each and then, finally, Cathal ran a hand over his face. "I can't believe that all my dreams of a new life for our people have come to this. When we stepped onto these shores, I thought a fresh start awaited us ... but I miscalculated. I've brought all of you to your doom."

Artair's dark gaze gleamed. He leaned forward, still holding Cathal's gaze fast. "It's not too late," he said, his voice low and firm. "Go before them tomorrow and surrender." Artair glanced then, down at the curtained alcove where wee Bhaltair still wailed like a banshee. "For our children."

"You're not seriously considering this, mac Calum?" Tormud's voice, rough with anger, drove a spike between the two brothers, severing the connection between them. "You'll not submit to those bastards?"

Cathal leaned back in his chair and did not answer for a few moments. Even though this was his forty-sixth winter, he usually felt invincible, as strong as men half his age. Not tonight though. This eve, after three tough days defending the fort, he felt every one of his years. His body, mind, and heart ached. He felt so incredibly tired.

"I don't want to let them beat us," he admitted finally, meeting Tormud's accusing gaze. The warrior had gone red in the face, his eyes gleaming in the light of a nearby cresset burning upon the wall. "But there comes a time when bravery turns into madness."

Tormud's face twisted. "You passed that point moons ago."

"Perhaps I did not realize it ... for tonight, with a newborn among us, I see clearly for the first time in a long while."

It was true. After Mor's disappearance and then betrayal, a fury unlike any other he had known ignited in his veins. Ever since, he felt as if he had been floundering around in the fog. But tonight, after another long day of battle, the mist had cleared—leaving him to see the situation as it really was.

Hopeless.

"You know we won't win this battle," Cathal said after a pause. "But you are even more stubborn than me about this, Tormud ... why?"

The Boar warrior glared back at him. He gripped the horn of mead so hard that his knuckles had turned bloodless. "This is the land of my birth," he growled out the words. "I'll not be forced off it."

"But you're a Boar, not an Eagle," Artair pointed out. "Dun Ringill never belonged to your people."

"When I left The Winged Isle, The Boar and The Eagle had settled into an uneasy alliance." Tormud's voice roughened as he continued. "But relations were never good. My own father was killed during a skirmish between our tribes, and my brother's wife ran off with an Eagle warrior." Tormud's face screwed up. "Dun Ringill is for them."

Cathal watched the warrior who had been his right-hand for many years now, realization dawning. He had never questioned Tormud's loyalty, yet had not understood that he'd had personal reasons for suggesting they take the tribe to The Winged Isle. He now saw that winning this fort had long been Tormud's dream—one that Cathal had helped him achieve.

He would not let go of that dream easily.

But it was no longer Cathal's dream. This great round-tower that looked west over the sea, where he had once hoped to grow old and fat, suddenly felt foreign and lonely.

He had lost nearly every person who had ever meant anything to him. He only had Artair left.

Cathal heaved in a deep breath then, exhaustion pulling him down in a dark undertow. It hurt to think, and yet a decision had to be made. "I will go before the chieftains of the united tribes tomorrow," he said finally. "And I will place us at their mercy." His gaze never left Tormud as he spoke, and he watched the warrior's expression darken. "Even if they take my head for it … they are likely to spare the women and children then."

Tormud lurched from his seat, mead sloshing over the rim of the horn he still gripped. Snarling, he hurled it away from him. Men and women in the hall below the platform turned, their gazes swiveling to where Tormud now glared at his chieftain.

"I never took you for a coward." Tormud choked the words out.

The insult washed over Cathal. He was too weary of the world to care tonight. And so he said nothing. He merely let Tormud issue a string of insults. Then the man turned and strode from the hall.

It was like watching a storm depart, and when The Boar had disappeared, Cathal sank back into his carven chair, despair washing through him.

Chapter Twenty-four

Freedom or Death

MOR PLUNGED THE cloth into the steaming water and sighed. The rough block of lye soap they had given her had flecks of rosemary in it. The scent wafted up, released by the heat of the water. Mor inhaled deeply, sluicing her face, neck, and breasts with hot water.

Now that she was no longer considered a prisoner, Galan's wife had brought her a wash bowl. She had also brought her clean clothes very similar to those she wore already: plaid leggings, a thick woolen tunic, and a leather vest.

The woman, tall and proud, with a wary gaze, had not engaged her in conversation, yet the kindness of the act had made Mor's vision blur. She had not bathed in many days. Her skin and scalp itched. She now knelt naked on the edge of the furs. She did not linger over the bathing. Someone might venture into the tent at any moment, and despite the burning brazier, the air in here held a chill.

Even so, Mor sighed in pleasure as she washed her long hair and massaged soap into her scalp before rinsing it clean. The scent of rosemary enveloped her, and she closed her eyes; it was the perfume of summer, reminding her of the small garden her mother had once tended.

Completing her bathing, Mor dressed in the clothes The Eagle chieftain's wife had brought. They fitted well, and Mor wondered if they had belonged to the woman herself. She was a tall, statuesque warrior woman, although not as tall as Mor. As such, the leggings were slightly too short in the leg. All the same, it felt wonderful to be clean again.

Mor was standing next to the brazier, teasing out the wet strands of her hair with her fingers to help it dry, when the tent flap drew back, and someone else entered. She had expected to see Galan's wife again, but instead it was Talor.

He carried a tray of food. Mor's heart leaped at the sight of him. Then her belly growled when her attention settled upon the tray bearing oatcakes, boiled eggs, butter, and cheese. A jug and two clay cups sat alongside the food.

Talor's mouth quirked. "Hungry?"

"Starving," Mor replied, careful to keep her expression aloof. She had been hoping to avoid Talor for the moment. He had been there earlier, had witnessed the entire scene with the chieftains, and listened while she spilled all her father's secrets afterward. The rosemary scented bath had distracted her for a brief time, but the sight of Talor brought everything back once more.

"Why are you here?" she asked softly.

Talor raised an eyebrow. "Isn't it obvious ... I'm about to have supper, and I'd like to share it with you." He nodded toward the furs. Please, sit down."

Moving away from the brazier, Mor did as bid. However, she still eyed the warrior cautiously. This was a side to Talor she had not yet seen—charming with a boyish edge that no doubt set many a lass's heart aflutter.

Is that why mine is beating so fast?

The Reaper take him, her pulse raced as if she had just finished a sprint.

Was this who Talor mac Donnel usually was, before grief and bitterness had driven him to Dun Ringill to kill her father ... a man who wore sensuality and self-confidence like a second skin?

He looked good tonight, dressed in leather breeches and a vest, his muscular arms left bare. He had shaved his jaw, and now that the bruises on his face had started to fade, the full force of his chiseled good-looks hit her.

Mor struggled to keep her breathing even and lowered herself onto the furs. Talor sat opposite her, twisting himself into a cross-legged position with ease and setting the wooden tray between them. He then poured them both cups of ale. "Don't mind me," he said with a slow smile that made Mor's breathing hitch. "Dig in."

Once again, Mor obeyed him. She spread butter upon a large oatcake and took a big bite, chewing fast, before she took another. Ever since she had been taken prisoner, her meals had been tiny and spaced far apart; they had not wanted to waste food on her.

But now that she would fight alongside them, she had earned the right to eat properly again.

"I'm surprised you dare visit this tent," Mor said as she swallowed the last of her oatcake and reached for an egg, which she began to peel. "Everyone here looks at me as if I am the bean-nighe."

Talor pulled a face at the comparison. The bean-nighe was a female spirit: an omen of death and a messenger from the Otherworld. Taking the form of an old woman, the bean-nighe was said to haunt desolate streams, washing the clothing of those about to die.

"A very attractive bean-nighe nonetheless," he replied, helping himself to a wedge of cheese.

Mor's fingers stumbled as she continued to peel her egg. Now he was flirting with her. She did not know what to say, how to respond to him. After everything that had happened that evening, she felt drained of words.

"A shadow lies across your eyes, Mor," Talor said when she did not answer his comment. "I don't like seeing you like this."

She raised her gaze, meeting his squarely for the first time since he had entered her tent. "I'm a traitor," she murmured, "I feel as if I don't belong anywhere now."

His brow furrowed. "Why did you offer all that information? I can see it has cost you."

Mor inhaled sharply, her gaze dropping to the egg. She finished peeling it but did not take a bite, considering her next words carefully. "For freedom, Talor. Whatever happens next, I want to face it as a free woman. The Serpent can only hold out for so long ... and when they fall, I don't want to still be a prisoner."

"It seems like a high price though." Talor reached for his cup of ale.

"Freedom or death," Mor replied, her tone flattening. "There's nothing in between. Would you have liked to have remained my father's prisoner? To be kicked and beaten, given scraps to eat, and then put to work cleaning privies before you slept with the dogs."

Talor took a draft of ale before meeting her gaze once more. "And you think we'll treat you this way?"

Mor held his gaze. "I know you would."

Talor's expression sharpened. "*I* wouldn't." He inclined his head then, his sea-blue eyes searching. "There's something else, Mor ... something you're not telling me. What is it?"

The Hag curse him. How had he sensed it?

She was so good at hiding her thoughts and feelings from others; few people suspected she withheld things. But not Talor. He saw right through her.

Mor's throat thickened. She could not confide in him though—it was too risky. No one could know what she was planning.

And so she shoved her urge to confide in him away and buried her feelings deep. "There is nothing else ... if I seem on edge, it is because I told you all my father's secrets. You know now that he hates being on the defensive. If cornered, he will attack. The moment you breach the gates, he and his warriors will come at you."

Talor nodded, his gaze hooding. "Aye … and we will put up ladders on the walls and attack him from behind."

Bile rose, stinging the back of Mor's throat. "Don't forget also that as soon as they are cornered, my father and his warriors will cast aside their swords and fight with daggers. They carry many strapped to their bodies. They will try to get as close as possible to you, and under your guards, before you can draw your own knives."

Talor continued to watch her. "And we will be ready."

Mor stared down at the egg she still held. She had been famished a few moments ago, yet now her belly churned. Self-loathing pulsed within her like a stoked ember. She had known that betraying her father would take its toll on her, but it hurt more than she expected. "How can you bear to be in my company," she finally managed. "A warrior does not betray their own … I deserve death, not freedom."

A beat of silence passed between them, and then Talor reached out, placing a hand over hers. The heat of his skin, the strength of his fingers, sent a blade of lust through Mor's lower belly; the sensation was so acute that she nearly gasped in response.

It had been like this from the moment of their first meeting—this pull, this attraction. One touch and her mind turned to porridge, and every nerve in her body grew taut.

"You're an incredible woman, Mor," he said, his fingers closing over hers. "Braver than anyone I've ever met. I look into your eyes, and I know you are a survivor. There's no one else's company I'd rather be in right now."

Mor's gaze flicked upward, meeting his once more. Her mouth lifted at the corners. "You have a honeyed tongue, Talor mac Donnel … I never realized just how charming you are … till today."

His mouth curved, and the sensuality of the expression made Mor's heart leap once more. Her skin

burned where he touched it, the sensation making her
incredibly aware of his nearness. She could feel the heat
of his body, reaching out and wrapping itself around her.
His hair was slightly damp, hinting that he too had
bathed this evening. He smelt of leather, mixed with a
spicy scent that was pure male. Mor's breathing
quickened, her nostrils flaring as she inhaled him.

"Aye ... you haven't seen this side of me," he admitted.
"Instead, you saw my ugly twin ... the man I'd rather
others didn't witness. You saw it all, and yet you don't
hate me as a result ... I don't know whether to be
impressed or alarmed."

Mor stared back at him, realizing what he was trying
to say. She had seen the worst of him—his hate and
vitriol—and yet she had still tried to help him and had
suffered his company. Likewise, he knew her to be a
traitor to her own father, and despite that, he was sitting
with her.

His fingers entwined with hers, and the uneaten egg
dropped onto the tray between them.

"I don't know what tomorrow will bring," Talor said
softly, "for either of us. All I know, Mor, is that from the
moment you appeared in my life, everything changed.
You burn as bright as a Gateway fire ... you draw me to
you. When I'm in your company, I like who I am. If I'm
no longer eaten up by a hunger for reckoning, it is your
doing. You bring out the best in me."

Mor's heart was beating so wildly now, she was sure
he must have been able to hear it. A wave of want swept
over her, dizzying in its intensity. "Do I?" she whispered
back, as her fingers tangled with his. Talor's thumb
brushed across her palm, and her breathing caught. "I
don't think I have that much influence over you."

"Aye, you do." Talor reached up with his free hand,
leaning forward as he cupped her face. "You have far
more power than you realize ... and if you would wield it,
there is little you couldn't achieve."

Chapter Twenty-five
Patience

MOR MOMENTARILY LOST the ability to speak. Instead, she merely stared back at Talor as he gazed into her eyes, his hand still cupping her cheek. Words deserted her. All she could focus on was the heat of his palm pressed against her skin.

The Mother preserve her, she had never known desire like this.

Need for Talor writhed in her belly. Despite their stillness, she sensed the lust that raged within him too—he held himself back, but his eyes had darkened to an inky blue, his pupils huge.

Energy crackled between them like the air before a violent storm.

Slowly, deliberately, Talor drew back from her. Then he picked up the tray and set it aside, placing it away from the furs so that nothing lay between them.

"You feel it too, don't you?" he asked. The rasp in his voice nearly undid her. The raw need that made her core ache for him. "This pull between us … it has been there from the beginning."

Mor nodded, not trusting herself to speak.

"I want to lose myself in you, Mor," he continued, his words weaving a spell around her. "I want to forget the rest of the world and everyone in it."

Mor's lips parted, a soft gasp escaping her. "I want …" she breathed, the word catching in her throat. "I want you so much … it scares me."

He shifted forward on his knees so that barely a hand-span lay between them on the furs. "I'm yours," he said, the words coming out in a low growl. "Take me."

And with those words, he released her from the last bindings of self-restraint. Before Mor knew what she was doing, she launched herself at him.

Talor was ready for her. They came together with a clash of lips, tongues, and teeth—a wild embrace that ended up with Mor sitting astride Talor. Her hands were everywhere, exploring the hard-muscled contours of his chest before sliding up to the bare skin of his neck. She did not know where to touch first. With a gasp, she dug her fingers through his short, thick hair, pushing herself hard against him as he slid his hands down the column of her back.

Their kisses softened. The first wave of desperate hunger had passed, and a soft mist of throbbing desire settled over Mor. Talor deepened his kisses, his tongue sliding against hers in a sensual caress that made Mor groan into his mouth. His hands cupped her buttocks then, and he drew her even closer to him. Mor felt the hard, throbbing heat of him pressed up against her, and despite that layers of clothing still separated them, shivers of pleasure rippled through her lower belly. Slowly, sensually, she rubbed herself against him, sliding up and down the magnificent length of his shaft.

In response, Talor groaned a curse against her mouth.

Reaching up, he began to unlace her leather vest. The movements were deft and efficient—and then the vest fell away.

Tearing her mouth from his, Mor leaned back, reached down, and caught the hem of the tunic she wore underneath. She pulled it up over her head, leaving the top half of her body naked to his hungry gaze. Glancing down, she saw that her breasts thrust toward him. They felt swollen and ached for his touch, his hot mouth. She had heavy breasts—an annoyance for a warrior woman, for she had to bind them carefully before battle lest they got in the way when she was fighting.

But Talor was not looking at them as if they were anything but beautiful.

His gaze gleamed, his lips parting. Then he leaned forward and captured a hard pink nipple in his mouth, suckling greedily.

The sensation made Mor gasp, and when he continued to suckle her, drawing her nipple deep into his mouth, she let out a soft whimper. The pleasure was exquisite—almost to the edge of pain. And when he gave her other breast the same treatment, Mor let her head fall back, a long, deep moan escaping her.

She was vaguely aware that if she made a noise, the two guards still stationed outside the tent, for her own safety now, might grow suspicious. But suddenly she did not care. All that mattered was that Talor did not stop what he was doing. She wanted to be naked with him here on the furs. She wanted him deep inside her.

"I need you," she groaned, digging her fingers into his scalp as she urged him on. "Now, Talor ... I can't wait."

He released her swollen nipple and drew back, his smile full of wicked promise. "Then I need to teach you some patience."

With that, he reached down and started to unlace her breeches.

With trembling hands, Mor undid his vest, pushing it off him to reveal the hard-muscled torso beneath. Bruises mottled his skin, many of them turning yellow as they faded; yet the healing injuries did not detract from the beauty of his body. The ache between Mor's thighs started to pulse.

She was not sure she could be patient. Tonight, she wanted to be greedy, to take whatever she wanted.

They wrestled out of the rest of their clothes, kicking their boots off, before Talor shoved Mor back on the furs and climbed over her.

Heart slamming against her ribs, Mor stared up at him and let her gaze travel boldly down the length of his body to where his rod thrust up from a matt of soft, dark hair toward her.

She reached down and stroked its length, feeling it grow harder still, pulsing under her grip.

Talor gasped, grabbed her wrists, and pulled her arms above her head, pinning them back against the furs. "Patience, mo leannan," he growled. "Keep that up, my lover, and things are going to be over too fast."

Mor let out a moan of frustration, her body arching up under him.

Releasing Mor's wrists, Talor started to kiss and lick his way down her body. He captured her swollen breasts once more, suckling them until her breathing came in short, panting gasps—and then he sat back on his heels, parted her thighs, and gazed down at the open heart of her.

"Beautiful," he whispered.

Gazing up at Talor, Mor saw that his high cheekbones were now flushed, his gaze was hooded, and his breathing came fast and shallow. Despite his teasing words, she could see that he was holding his control by a tight leash.

Spreading her legs wider still, he started to stroke her between them. He watched Mor's face as he did so, hungry for her reaction. He knew how to touch her too, arrowing the pad of his thumb over the most sensitive spot so that within moments Mor was whimpering and gasping under his touch.

"Talor," she moaned, shuddering as a wave of pleasure crested and washed over her. "Oh Gods ... please."

He gave a soft laugh but did not stop, and when he slid a finger deep inside her, Mor was so highly sensitized that she cried out, arching up against him.

Eyes flickering open, she saw that he still watched her, his face taut with a feral hunger that caused something dark and wild to stir inside her.

"Take me!" she gasped. "Don't be gentle. Plow me so hard that I scream."

Her words made his breathing still for a heartbeat. Talor let out a filthy curse and shifted back from between her thighs. Grasping hold of her hips he flipped Mor over, raising her up on all fours.

Excitement caught fire in Mor's loins. She could feel his hot gaze raking over her naked buttocks. His hand stroked the curve of them, before he nudged her thighs farther apart with his knee.

And then she felt it—the tip of his shaft—hot and hard against her.

Without any warning, Talor slid into her, sheathing himself to the hilt in one deep, claiming thrust.

Mor's cry filled the tent, aching pleasure slamming into her. Her body trembled and convulsed from the force of it. If his hands had not been grasping her hips, her legs would have given way under her. As he took her, Talor reached forward and grasped her hair. He tangled his fingers in it, drawing her head back so that her body stretched, taut as a drawn bow-string. It was a dominant gesture, and it excited Mor beyond measure.

It was too much. She had told him to plow her hard, but she was not sure if she could take any more pleasure than this.

"Talor," she gasped, curling her fingertips into the furs. "I don't know if—"

Another deep thrust choked the words out of her— and another, and another. He took her hard, sliding deeper into her each time. He was doing as she had bid, and Mor gripped the furs now, anchoring herself as pleasure crashed over her, flattening her. Being taken like this was incredible; he touched places inside her she had never known existed.

She cried out—the sound raw—and then there was nothing but her sobbing gasps, Talor's ragged breathing, and the slap of their flesh meeting with each powerful thrust.

Talor plowed her hard, reducing Mor to a trembling wreck. Tears of pleasure trickled down her face, and she gave herself up to it, let herself fly like a loosed arrow. And when he gave one last deep thrust, his body going rigid against hers, she heard Talor's loud groan of pleasure, felt the tremors that went through his body— and he collapsed against her, spent.

Chapter Twenty-six

Repaid in Blood

"YOU'VE RUINED ME for other women," Talor murmured into Mor's ear. He held her close, spooning against her, their legs entwined. "You do realize that?"

She gave a soft, sensual laugh. "You're not a stranger to the pleasures of the furs, are you, Talor?"

He huffed. "What's that supposed to mean?"

"Exactly that." Her voice was soft, sleepy, and laced with amusement. "Something tells me you've never been short of female attention."

"I can't help it if women throw themselves at me."

Mor sighed. "The Reaper's cods, you're arrogant. Lucky for you, I like cocky men."

A grin spread across Talor's face. "And I like warrior women who turn into wolves in the furs," he murmured in her ear. He felt a shiver pass through her at these words, and his grin widened.

He loved how responsive Mor was. How his touch turned her wild. She had insinuated that he knew his way around a woman's body—and he did—but a woman like this brought out the best in a man. Mor had given herself entirely to him, had encouraged him with groans, cries, and lusty words. She had no inhibitions. There was something incredibly sensual about a woman who owned her own pleasure, who knew what she wanted from a man and was not afraid to take it.

He had not been lying. How could he ever couple with another woman? Any other would be but a pale shadow in comparison to this fire-haired beauty. Over the years, he had suspected that some of the women he had lain with found him a little 'too much'. He had a large appetite for sensual pleasure, and one or two of his lovers had been exhausted by it.

Not Mor though—he had the sense that they had only scratched the surface when it came to what was possible between them.

Talor's smile faded then. Mor had fallen silent, and he could tell from the way her body relaxed that she was on the edge of letting sleep claim her. Would they ever get this chance again?

Tonight was special. Tonight, Mor had been given leave to fight alongside her former enemy for a day. But when Dun Ringill fell, everything would change. Since Cathal had not surrendered, the warriors of the united tribes would not treat any survivors of the siege kindly. Talor had seen what could happen after battle. Warriors were capable of anything when their blood was up. There would be rape, torture, and more killing.

What will happen to Mor?

A fierce wave of protection swept over Talor then, causing him to tighten his grip around his lover. The chieftains had given Mor her freedom; after the battle ended she would be able to make a new life for herself here. But Talor knew how deep the hate went for the people of The Serpent. It did not matter what promises had been made, Mor would not be safe after the siege ended.

He already knew that he would not let anyone touch Mor. She was capable of defending herself, but if any of the chieftains decided that she was no longer welcome among them, he would not hesitate to stand at her side.

Talor's pulse quickened at the thought.

He had never felt like this before. Aye, he was highly protective of his own kin, but this instinct to look after Mor caught him off guard. She had teased him earlier, told him he was honey-tongued when he had complimented her—and yet he had meant every word.

Somehow, she had changed him. She had helped free him of a prison of his own making. She had done something that he would never have—she had gone to the enemy and put her own neck on the line in the pursuit of peace.

Only, it had all gone wrong for her. He was sorry about that. Sorry that she would have to see her own people fall the following day.

Leaning forward, Talor placed a tender kiss on Mor's neck. She murmured softly, on the verge of falling asleep. He did not want to wake her, and so he enfolded Mor in his arms and buried his face in her neck. She smelled sweet, and the scent of rosemary wafted up, enfolding him.

Usually, after taking a woman so vigorously, fatigue would crash over him, and he would sleep deeply.

Not so tonight. It grew late now, and outdoors the camp slumbered. But sleep eluded Talor. Many warriors had again set a watch around the perimeter, and if Talor had not been here with Mor, he would have joined them. But he would not leave his lover's side, would not break the enchantment of this moment.

The silence drew out, and Mor's breathing deepened. Yet Talor remained awake, holding her tight until the first glimmer of dawn filtered into the tent.

Cathal mac Calum emerged from the broch, his gaze traveling east to where the sun was rising.

The snow, which had been their ally over the past days, had stopped now. The clear sky to the east warned him that the enemy would have the advantage now. There was little warmth in the sun, and it would take a while for the snow to thaw. Nevertheless, it tipped the scales even further toward the besiegers.

Cathal heaved in a deep breath before exhaling slowly.

He had barely slept all night, wrestling with the hardest decision of his life. But in the end, he had made up his mind.

The birth last night had awoken him to how much he loved his people. He had lost his wife and children, but he still had many men, women, and children within these walls who would follow him unquestioningly anywhere.

If the siege continued today, all of them would die. He knew it in his bones.

Descending the steps, The Serpent chieftain cast a gaze over the crowd of men and women awaiting him. Tall and proud, they watched him approach, awaiting his instruction. Cathal saw the wariness upon their faces and wondered if Tormud had already spoken to some of them. However, the wariness could also be because all of them knew that today they would fight their last.

They were brave and loyal—but they would not charge toward death without a flicker of hesitation.

This realization made Cathal clench his jaw, resolve filtering over him.

Walking into their midst, he swept his gaze over the surrounding crowd. There were barely a hundred and fifty of them left now. The enemy archers had been skilled; they had taken more of his warriors down from the walls than he had anticipated.

"The time has come," Cathal spoke, his gruff voice ringing across the frozen yard between the broch and the high wall that protected them from the outside world. "We stand on the edge of a great gulf."

No one answered him. Instead, they watched their chieftain, a tense silence falling over the crowd.

"You have followed me across the seas," Cathal continued, raising his voice so that even those at the back could hear every word. He did not want any of them to miss this. He would not say it twice. "You have fought at my side through countless campaigns. There are no warriors braver than those who stand before me. None with bigger hearts."

Cathal's throat thickened then. He did not know what was wrong with him.

Maybe it was Mor's betrayal. Being stripped of everything had left him vulnerable. His family had been his shield; he had not needed anyone's approval, just as long as his sons and daughter fought at his side.

But all had turned to ashes now.

He stood alone—these warriors before him were all he had left. Of course, he had Artair. But his brother was crippled from his injuries and would wait out the battle from inside the broch. The pair of them had always fought together until now, often side by side, as they hacked their way through a battlefield.

That day would never come again.

"You have stood with me, and I have repaid you in blood," Cathal said finally, his voice roughening. It was difficult to admit this to his people, and yet he had to say it, he had to be honest with them. "But this morning it all ends. I will go now before the chieftains of the united tribes—I will kneel before them and ask that they spare what is left of my people."

Cathal's gaze swept over their faces once more, taking in the shock, the anger, and the grief he saw there. Most wore worried expressions, while one or two looked visibly relieved. "Many of you will not understand this decision," he continued, "but know that I am doing this for you all. This is the only way to ensure that the people of The Serpent have a chance at survival."

Cathal shifted his attention to the cluster of warriors who stood before the walls. "Unbar the gates," he ordered. "I will go out to them ... on foot and alone."

A moment of stunned silence passed and then, after exchanging glances, the warriors moved aside.

The clunk and grate of iron against wood filled the chill morning air. Around Cathal, no one spoke. All the same, he could feel their gazes upon him. Ignoring the crowd now, The Serpent chieftain moved toward the gates. They would only need to open one a few feet for him to be able to slip through. Cathal walked toward the rapidly widening gap. He carried no weapons this morning, and felt naked without his heavy sword at his hip and his shield slung across his back.

But he had to go before the enemy unarmed. He could not kneel before them bearing weapons.

A white world appeared before him through the gap, the dawn light sparkling.

Cathal was only two paces away from the gate when something hit him hard between the shoulder-blades.

He grunted, his breath gusting out of him, and staggered forward. Pain sledge-hammered into him, exploding across his upper back—and then something hit him again. The wet ripping sound of iron against flesh split the morning's stillness.

Gods ... I've been stabbed.

Cathal staggered again and went down on his knees. Agony ripped across his chest and then, suddenly, he retched up blood.

His vision darkened as he coughed and choked, before a pair of bulky boots and thick leather clad legs stepped in front of him. A rough hand grabbed hold of his hair and yanked his head up.

Cathal craned his neck, his gaze meeting Tormud mac Alec's.

The Boar's face was twisted in a rictus of hate, while around him the world had gone still. No one rushed to their chieftain's aid; no one tried to intercept Tormud.

"Did you really think I'd let you surrender?" Tormud snarled, giving Cathal's head a shake as if he was a dog he was teaching a lesson.

Cathal did not reply. Instead, he hacked up a mouthful of blood. He could not breathe. His ears were starting to ring; Tormud's voice sounded as if it reached him from the end of a long tunnel.

Rage swept through Cathal, raking its vicious claws across his heart. He was furious at himself for not anticipating this move from Tormud.

Old Murdina had spoken of a traitor, that someone in his inner circle would betray him. He had thought it was Mor, but as Tormud let go of his hair and he fell forward onto the blood-splattered snow, he realized he had been wrong.

The one who would turn on him was the man he had trusted like his own brother over the years. Tormud wanted control of this tribe as much as he wanted control of Dun Ringill—and Cathal had been too blind to see it.

Cold, slushy snow crushed against his face, and Cathal's eyes fluttered shut as darkness took him.

Chapter Twenty-seven

Twisting the Blade

MOR CLIMBED THE ladder, following Talor, Muin, and other warriors up onto the wall. She had just reached the top when the gates gave way with a screech of rending iron. A great shout went up outside the walls, the cries of men and women echoing into the clear noon sky.

The attack had recommenced shortly after dawn— and although her father's warriors had done their best to hold back the tide, the inevitable had occurred. They had broken through.

Mor's pulse hammered in her ears as she joined Talor. Together the pair of them looked back at the gates, at where warriors now surged in to meet those defending the fort.

And as she had predicted, her father moved those warriors on the walls down to the gates.

With a sharp nod to Talor and Mor, Muin followed the others and moved away toward the steep stairs leading down to the yard below. Silently, Mor and Talor trailed behind them.

Although she had seen Muin mac Galan a number of times since her capture, Mor had not been properly introduced to him until that morning. She had emerged from the tent with Talor at her side to find Muin waiting for them. Arms folded across his broad chest, the warrior had cast them a look that was both knowing and exasperated. "I thought I might find my cousin here."

The wail of a hunting horn boomed off the walls of Dun Ringill.

Mor descended the stairs, drawing the long blade she carried strapped to her thigh. Her heart was now pounding so loudly that nausea crept over her. Usually, bloodlust caught hold of her as soon as her father's horn echoed through the ranks of warriors. But today no sense of elation swelled within her. Mor's decision to join the enemy ranks had merely been a ruse to get inside Dun Ringill, yet it felt wrong all the same.

But she did not shrink back from it. She had set out on this path the moment she had freed Talor. She would not waver now.

Nonetheless, as Muin and his companions clashed with Cruthini up ahead, the sense of wrongness within Mor grew.

These were her people. If she was with the enemy, she would have to draw her sword and attack—but she could not bear to harm them. When she had planned ahead, she had glossed over this detail.

As if sensing her conflict, Talor placed a hand upon Mor's arm.

"Keep back," he instructed. "If I need you, I'll let you know."

She pulled against his grip. "I can't let you face them alone."

He threw her a wolfish grin. "Worry not ... Muin will watch my back."

And with that, he released her arm and strode forward, drawing two fighting knives as he went.

Mor watched him go, her hand tightening around the hilt of her knife. She could not just stand here watching while he fought. And yet she knew what he was doing—

he was trying to protect her from having to spill her own people's blood.

He did not want her to live with more regret than she did already. She had put up a brave front standing before the chieftains, but Talor had seen through it.

However, he did not realize that he had just unwittingly helped her move one step further to her goal.

Mor was never one to shy away from a fight. She knew she was not a coward, and yet she backed away from where the warriors now battled each other. As she stepped into the shadow of the wall, never taking her gaze from where Talor slashed and stabbed at his opponent, a fresh group of warriors—these ones bearing the mark of The Boar upon their biceps—rushed past and launched themselves into the fray.

Drawing in a deep breath, and trying to quell the nausea that roiled within her, Mor let her attention shift from Talor, scanning the crowd for a sign of her father.

It was time to make her move.

Her plan hinged on finding her father—and quickly.

Cathal mac Calum was usually easy to spot. A big man, he stood out with his wild auburn hair and magnetic presence. Yet, one sweep of the crowd, and she knew he was not there.

The sense of wrongness Mor had felt upon scaling the wall intensified. Maybe it was not due to her guilt about fighting her own people at all, and instead to do with her father.

She needed to find him.

Leaving her watching place by the wall, Mor sheathed her knife for the moment, skirted the yard, and rushed up the stairs to the broch. She barged toward two warriors guarding the door. The men's gazes flew wide at the sight of their chieftain's daughter. Mor recognized them both—neither of them were men she was fond of. Then they launched themselves forward, grappling for her.

Mor flattened one with a punch to the jaw, before elbowing his companion in the belly and sending him toppling down the stairs.

A heartbeat later Mor slammed her shoulder against the door, only to find it bolted shut from the inside. She hammered her fists against it. "It's me, Mor," she shouted. "Let me in, Da!"

"Cathal mac Calum won't answer you, lass," a voice rasped behind her.

Mor twisted, drawing her knife once more as she did so. There, a few steps below her, stood Tormud mac Alec.

"And why's that?" she asked, her voice turning chill. She had forgotten how much she disliked this man, how the feel of his gaze raking over her body made her want to sink a blade into his belly.

"Because he's dead."

Ice pooled within Mor, and she went still. Around her the sounds of fighting faded. The world receded so that she and Tormud were the only ones present.

"You killed him." It was a statement, not a question. She knew from the gleam in the warrior's eye, and the fact that her father was not in the midst of the fighting, that Tormud had betrayed him.

A smile stretched Tormud's lips. "Aye. The craven dog was about to surrender to the enemy." He advanced toward her, taking each step slowly. He carried a thin-bladed knife in his right hand, his body coiled for action. "Like you already have, you deceitful whore."

Fury coiled up within Mor, a wild and dangerous emotion that snaked through her breast and sent heat pulsing out through her limbs. "You murdered a man who saw you as a brother," she growled.

"It's no worse than his own daughter running off with the enemy," Tormud countered. "You sank the first knife into him on that day ... I merely twisted the blade."

With a roar, Mor rushed at him. Her knife-blade flashed, but Tormud was ready for her. They had sparred plenty of times; he knew she was lethal with a blade, but he also knew how she fought, and so anticipated the attack.

Leaping to one side, Tormud let Mor lunge past him. She tripped on the steps and fell forward, colliding with the warrior she had pushed down the steps earlier. The man, who had just been trying to get up, went down once more, cushioning her fall.

Mor rolled to her feet, bending her knees as Tormud reached the bottom of the stairs. He tossed his knife before casting her an arrogant smile. "Have you enjoyed your time with Talor mac Donnel?" he sneered. "I bet you didn't waste any time spreading your legs for him."

Mor ignored the taunt. He wanted her to answer, he wanted to goad her into losing her temper and doing something rash. He had never forgiven her for spurning his advances. He intended to kill her for it.

But now that she had weathered the initial surge of rage, calmness settled over Mor.

Finally, her battle fury was upon her—that place she entered in the midst of chaos. Around her the fight for Dun Ringill raged. Talor was somewhere in the midst of it all, yet she could not tear her attention away from Tormud in order to look for him. She had to keep present and focused.

Tormud had to die—and she would be the one to bring him down.

And with this last thought, she drew a small knife that she wore strapped to her left thigh and threw it at the warrior's throat. It embedded with a dull, meaty thud.

Tormud had not expected that move.

He had thought she would launch herself at him again, that she would try to sink her blade under his ribs or armpit, as was her usual fighting style. But he had forgotten that Mor knew how to throw knives—with both hands.

The Boar warrior staggered back, one hand going up to grip the hilt of the blade she had just thrown. He then yanked it free—a mistake, for blood sprayed from the wound. Tormud's eyes bulged, and he staggered again, the blade he carried in his other hand clattering to the ground. He raised both hands to his wounded neck to try and stem the bleeding.

Mor was on him in an instant. The knife she still gripped in her right hand slid up under his ribs, driving through his leather vest and deep into his flesh. Tormud crumpled, and Mor sank to her knees with him, her gaze never leaving his.

"This is for my father," she snarled.

Tormud's mouth worked, blood trickling down his chin, and then she watched the life seep from his dark eyes, felt the fight go out of his body. He collapsed upon the ground, eyes staring sightlessly up at the sky.

Breathing hard, Mor pulled the knife free from Tormud's ribs.

She realized then that while she had been facing her father's killer, the fighting around her had subsided. Serpent warriors lay scattered around the yard, many dead and some injured or subdued. She watched as a few yards away, Galan of The Eagle pressed a knee between a man's shoulder-blades, pinning him to the ground. The Eagle chieftain's iron-grey gaze swept across the yard then, resting upon Mor.

"Where's your father?" Galan ground out, out of breath from the fighting.

"Dead." Mor's belly twisted as she said the word. "Tormud slew him before the battle began ... he was going to surrender."

Silence followed her words, punctuated only by the groans of the injured.

Galan's gaze shifted to the dead man sprawled before Mor. "And that's Tormud?"

"Aye."

Talor approached her then, picking his way through the dead. He was blood-splattered and sweat-slicked but appeared unhurt. Nearing Mor, Talor reached out a hand. Wordlessly, she took it and rose to her feet. In the aftermath of killing Tormud, her body suddenly felt weak, and a chill that had nothing to do with the bitter season stole through her limbs.

"Are you injured?" Talor asked when she leaned against him, his brows knitting together in concern.

Mor shook her head.

She noted then that Varar of The Boar, Tadhg of The Stag, and Wid of The Wolf approached. Their faces were hard, their gazes still gleaming with battle madness.

The chill seeped into Mor's veins, and she suppressed a shiver.

Galan secured the fallen Serpent warrior's wrists behind his back, before he too rose to his feet, stepping up next to Varar.

Mor faced them. "Did you hear what I said?" she murmured, her throat suddenly dry and scratchy. "My father was ready to lay down arms, to negotiate with you ... this last battle would have never happened if Tormud hadn't murdered him."

"That doesn't matter now," Varar, The Boar chieftain, replied. His voice was low and flat, his gaze pitiless. "The tide has turned in our favor. Your people have raped our isle ... and anyone left alive in that broch must suffer the consequences."

Chapter Twenty-eight

What is Written is Written

MOR WAS ABOUT to answer Varar, to argue with him, when the heavy door to the broch above them swung open. Twisting around, Mor's gaze alighted upon a well-built man with short auburn hair, leaning upon a wooden crutch.

Her heart leaped into her throat.

Artair.

Why had he opened the door to the attackers? Surely, he knew what would befall those still alive inside the broch—the women and children that were all that remained of her people. If he had kept the door closed, he could have ensured their safety for a short while longer at least, he could have given her time to diffuse the anger of the four chieftains before her.

Mor's uncle wore a grave expression as his gaze swept across the devastation in the yard before the broch. He would have expected as much, and yet Mor saw the grief that shadowed his green eyes, the tension that emanated from his once strong warrior's body.

With an effort, Artair navigated the stone steps, slowly descending them, wincing from discomfort as he went. Halfway down, he stopped.

"Thirty women, children, and old folk wait inside the broch," he said finally, a rasp to his voice. "And I, a cripple, am all that stands in your way." Artair's voice echoed across the yard. "You can cut me down and slaughter them, or you can finish this bloodshed between our peoples now."

"You started this," Wid mac Manus shouted. "My son now rots under a cairn of stones thanks to your people."

"Killing the rest of us won't bring him back," Artair replied. "I too lost kin in this fight."

"It'll give me reckoning," Wid snarled, advancing toward the bottom of the steps. Mor saw then that The Wolf chieftain carried a blood-stained sword. His gaze blazed with hate.

Heart hammering, Mor glanced back at her uncle. Artair was unarmed and crippled from his injuries—yet he was a warrior to the core. He stared down at Wid, defiant. Artair would not be stepping aside. The Wolf chieftain would have to kill him if he wanted to enter the broch.

"A bairn was born here last night," Artair said, his attention never wavering from Wid. "The first of our people to be born upon this isle. Would you take that new life? Would you redden your hands with his blood?"

Wid snarled. Instead of making him hesitate, Artair's words had merely inflamed his rage further. Spitting out a curse, Wid lunged forward.

Mor tore herself from Talor's side and blocked his path. "No, Wid," she gasped out the words. "Please stop this. You've had your vengeance."

They stared at each other, and Mor cast aside the knife she still held, leaving herself unarmed before The Wolf chieftain. It was a risky move, for she could see he was maddened by rage. He could decide to cut her down before he dealt with Artair—yet that was a risk she was willing to take.

The last stage of her plan finally fell into place.

When she had offered to fight alongside these people, it had been with this end in mind. She would beg to save the lives of those inside the keep, even if she lost her own in the process.

"Mor." Talor's voice was tight with alarm and held a warning note. "Step aside."

Mor refused to look at him, refused to shift her attention from Wid.

"This must end now," she said, her voice falling. "Take my life if you have to." She lowered herself onto her knees before him. "Strike me down in retribution for everyone you have lost ... but spare the lives of those who have never raised arms against you." Her voice hitched as she said these last words. "I beg you."

Wid stared at her. His face was all hard angles, and a nerve twitched in his cheek. She could tell that violent emotion raged beneath the surface, that he was hanging onto his self-control by the merest thread.

It was a reckless thing she had just done.

Mor could feel Talor's gaze boring into her, but still she did not look his way. He would be angry with her for risking her life like this.

But he did not understand how she truly felt. The fate of her people was at stake here. She would not step aside.

"Are you mad, woman?" Wid's voice held a rasp. "Why would you sacrifice yourself?"

"Because these are my people."

"I thought you had agreed to fight alongside us?"

"I did ... but Dun Ringill has fallen now. I won't stand by and watch anyone else die."

"She's right." Talor spoke up then, his voice low and wary. "The fort has fallen ... let us lower our weapons."

And then, to Mor's infinite surprise, Talor stepped up next to her. The thud of his knives falling to the ground filled the now silent yard. Mor chanced a glance away from Wid then, craning her neck up, her gaze taking in Talor's proud profile. He watched The Wolf chieftain with a calm, yet resolute expression.

She knew then that he would not leave her side—no matter what happened.

"This isn't how it's supposed to end," Talor continued. His attention shifted from Wid and slid over the faces of the other chieftains who looked on, stone-faced. "Don't you remember? Ailene cast the bones at Mid-Winter Fire and told us that The Eagle and The Serpent would be united in the future."

Muttering followed these words, as a few of the surrounding warriors exchanged glances. A few yards away, Mor saw Talor's cousin, Muin, tense.

Mor frowned, remembering that Ailene—the bandruí of The Eagle had foreseen the same as Old Murdina.

Talor looked down at Mor, his mouth curving in a rueful smile. "Aye … two bandruí can't be wrong, can they?" He paused then, focusing on the crowd that amassed around them. A few feet away, Wid had gone dangerously still, his fingers flexing around the hilt of his sword.

Mor tensed. The Wolf chieftain was just moments away from springing at her.

"You should all know that after Mor helped me escape, we visited her tribe's seer … an old woman who now resides in the cave just south of Dun Ringill," Talor continued, seemingly oblivious to the tension that now crackled through the air. "Old Murdina read the entrails of a stoat and told us that the only way our peoples can be united is by marriage between Mor and myself. She only had to set eyes on Mor and me to know the truth that it has taken me till now to acknowledge."

Talor turned to Mor, ignoring everyone else. And then, to her shock, he lowered himself onto one knee before her, so their eyes were level. "You were made for me, Mor of The Serpent. You have gone against your own in an effort to bring peace between our peoples, and now I stand against my own to do the same."

Shocked whispers rippled around them, yet Mor was unable to look away from Talor. Instead, she drowned in the blue fire of his eyes.

"You are mine, Mor," he said huskily, "and I am yours. And if you will be my wife, we will unite our peoples."

"Enough of this!" Wid lunged forward then—but to Mor's shock, Tadhg of The Stag and Galan of The Eagle caught hold of his arms and hauled him back. During the exchange, the two chieftains had moved closer to Wid.

The Wolf chieftain's roar echoed through the yard, ricocheting off the stone walls of the broch. "Bastards … let me go!"

"Calm down, Wid," Galan growled, his grip never loosening. "See past your anger for a moment and listen, would you?"

"Aye … fury won't help you now," Tadhg added. Despite that Wid was broad and strong, both Tadhg and Galan held him easily. The Stag chieftain's brow was furrowed as he stared at Talor. "And neither will rash decisions. Are you sure this is what you want, lad?"

"It doesn't matter what he wants," a woman's voice cut in then. "What is written is written. To go against the will of the Gods is foolish indeed."

The crowd parted then, and a small wizened figure swathed in thick furs emerged. Mor's breathing hitched. Old Murdina had ventured from her cave and come to them. Another woman—this one young and dark-haired, with lines of woad smeared across her cheeks—walked with Murdina, allowing the crone to rest upon her arm. Ailene, the bandruí of The Eagle, had left the encampment in the wake of the battle.

Together, the seers had visited them.

A shocked silence settled over the yard. The victors and the defeated alike grew still, their gazes settling upon the two women who stood before them. Even Wid stopped struggling, his gaze growing wide.

Watching the tension upon The Wolf chieftain's face, Mor reflected just how much power the bandruís wielded among their people. These women were a conduit between this world and the next, between mortals and the Gods. Their divinations directed the future, and could break or make lives.

"Is this true then?" Artair asked, splintering the weighty hush. Mor's uncle watched Old Murdina intently. "Have you read that this is the way?"

The crone nodded, before she cast a sly look at the woman beside her. "We have both seen it."

All gazes settled upon Ailene then. The young bandruí's face was stern, yet her blue eyes gleamed as her attention fixed upon Talor. He was still on one knee next to Mor.

"Mor told me what Murdina foretold," she said softly. "But I sought to hear the full divination myself. You should have told me everything the moment you arrived at the camp, Talor ... it would have made things easier for us all."

"We thought you wouldn't believe us," Talor replied, holding his cousin's gaze. "And in truth, it wasn't something I wanted to accept myself." He broke off there, his attention swinging back to Mor. The intensity on his face made her breathing quicken. "Until recently."

"A seer can be wrong," Wid growled.

"Aye ... even the best of you can misread the omens," Varar added. The Boar chieftain had kept silent during the discussion. However, he was scowling now. Unlike Tadhg and Galan, he had not stepped up to stop Wid. Watching him, Mor sensed the conflict in the chieftain.

Like Wid, he wanted retribution. The Boar had suffered greatly in this war, and although Varar had won back An Teanga, his people had been decimated by the invasion. It would take a long while for them to grow strong again.

"They did not misread about *us*." Another woman appeared, pushing her way through the edge of the crowd. Fina's face was grave as she crossed to Varar's side and stood beside him. "If Ailene's prediction could bring The Eagle and The Boar together, why would she be wrong about The Eagle and The Serpent?"

"I told you to keep away from the fort," Varar muttered, his gaze narrowing.

"The fighting is done," his wife countered with an irritated wave of her hand. "I'm with bairn, Varar ... not made of eggshell." Fina's attention shifted across to Ailene then. "How sure are you of your prediction?"

The bandruí's jaw firmed, her shoulders straightening. "I cast the bones again this morning," she replied. "They continue to tell me the same thing ... that there will be a union. The bloodshed ends today."

Chapter Twenty-nine

The Bloodshed Ends Today

TALOR LISTENED TO his cousin speak, and the fear that had clamped his chest in a vise from the moment that Mor had leaped out in front of Wid eased just a little.

He was a warrior to the core. Joy flowed through him every time he unsheathed his weapons and went into battle. But the past few days had changed Talor, had made him view life from a different perspective.

His uncle Galan had once told him that hatred was like a serpent devouring its own head—an endless cycle that would never stop as long as you fed the beast. Glancing across at his uncle now, Talor knew that Galan would be the easiest of the four chieftains to convince. Galan mac Muin had spent his life striving for peace, and more often than not failing.

But today that could all change.

"Maybe some good can come from all of this," he spoke up, focusing now on Wid's glowering face, before his gaze flicked to Varar. The Boar chieftain still wore a hard, guarded expression. "Before the Cruthini landed upon our shores we were divided ... suspicious of each other. But they united us, brought down the barriers that have kept us at each other's throats for years. They made all of the grievances we had against each other seem petty."

"Are you saying we should thank them?" Wid spat out the words. He was red in the face now and panting from the force of his outrage.

"No," Talor countered. "All I'm saying is that the future is now ours to shape as we wish." His gaze narrowed as it held Wid's. "You once hated The Eagle. My people killed scores of yours. After Galan and Tea wed, you could have decided to carry on the feud, but instead you decided to put our history behind you. Why can't you do that again?"

A nerve flickered under Wid's left eye as he stared back at Talor. "They killed my son," he rasped. "I miss Bred with every waking breath."

"As I miss Bonnie," Talor replied softly. "And yet I am willing to let the past go."

Another silence settled across the yard, broken by a bairn's wail inside the broch. The cry was lusty, life-affirming—the squalling of a newborn hungry for its mother's teat. The skin on Talor's forearms prickled as he listened.

Wid heard it too, and as Talor watched him, the man's face crumpled, tears leaking down his cheeks. There was no need for Talor to say another word, the infant's crying had driven his point home.

The Wolf chieftain sagged in Tadhg and Galan's arms, and when Talor glanced back at Varar, he saw that his friend's face had softened too, his gaze now shadowed.

The danger that had crackled in the air between them all dissolved now, and for the first time Talor was aware of the gentle kiss of the noon sun bathing his face.

He turned then to Mor and saw that she had risen to her feet. He raised his chin to meet her eye once more.

"Are you going to get off your knees now?" she asked, a husky edge to her voice.

Talor shook his head. He had not planned to throw himself between Wid and Mor, but at a certain point during their confrontation, something had splintered within him—the last shield that had kept him from facing the truth.

Mor had only been part of his life for a few days, and yet he could not bear the thought of continuing without her. The way she was prepared to sacrifice herself for her people, the brave way she faced death squarely without even flinching, made him want her even more than he already did.

He could search the whole world and never meet anyone like her again.

"There is a saying upon this isle," he said finally. *"Your feet will bring you to where your heart is ...* I never realized it, but from the moment I came into this world, my path was leading me to you."

Old Murdina had spoken true. It was written. He and Mor had been destined for each other. He was tired of fighting fate, fighting what he knew to be the right choice.

Mor's eyes gleamed. "So, this was always meant to be then?"

"Aye ... you didn't have a chance to answer me before," he replied, his mouth curving. "Will you be my wife, Mor?"

She stared at him, before a tear escaped and trickled down her cheek. Even so, it felt like an eternity to Talor before she replied.

"Gladly," Mor whispered.

A strange calm settled over Dun Ringill in the aftermath of the siege. Talor had noted such an atmosphere before. After the din and chaos of battle, the world always seemed to grow still and watchful. It was a time for reflection, a time to grieve for those lost—even for the victors.

Stepping inside Dun Ringill for the first time in many moons, Talor's breath caught. The Serpent survivors had been emptied out of the broch—they would reside for the time being in the village beyond until a decision was made about their future. In the days to come, The Wolf, The Stag, and The Boar would return home, but for the moment they remained at Dun Ringill, and the chieftains and their kin took the alcoves that lined the feasting hall inside the broch, while their warriors slept upon the rush-strewn floor.

"It looks bigger than I remember." Fina stepped up to Talor's shoulder, her arm snaking around his waist as she hugged him tight.

Talor tore his gaze from his surroundings and cast her a smile. "Aye ... we were getting cramped at Balintur ... it doesn't look as though The Serpent damaged anything."

A few yards away, warriors heaved a fresh lump of peat onto the great fire pit that warmed the space. Men and women filled the broch, and yet the mood was subdued. Talor had expected more festivity, more excitement, at getting their broch back—but mostly he just saw relief and fatigue on the faces surrounding him.

"I'm glad it's over," he murmured. "I just wish Bonnie had lived to see us back here."

"She's still with us," Fina replied, squeezing him against her once more. "I felt her presence this morning, standing at my side as I watched you launch your last attack at the gates. A soft smile graced her lips then, her grey eyes misting. "Listen to me ... it must be the bairn ... I'm not usually so weepy."

Talor smiled back, his throat constricting. He understood how his cousin felt though; being back here again had moved him more than he had thought it would. Standing inside this broch brought back so much—memories of when Bonnie had been with them. Still, he liked the idea of her watching over them as they went into battle, the idea that although her body lay beneath a cairn of stones, her soul flew free.

Talor slung an arm around Fina's shoulders and led her toward the chieftain's table, where platters of food were being set out for supper. It had been a long, exhausting day, and Talor had spent most of it helping to clear out the bodies of the dead. Repairs had already begun on the gates and walls, although it would take many days for all signs of the siege to be erased from Dun Ringill.

Fina stepped away from Talor and joined Varar at the table. Husband and wife shared a long and tender look, before Varar handed her a cup of milk. A few feet away, Muin wrapped a protective arm around Ailene's shoulders, while she leaned into him, smiling at something he had just said.

Warmth filtered over Talor at seeing all three of his cousins so happy. It had been a hard year, the most difficult of his life, and it had tested them all to the limit. But they had emerged stronger—and hopefully wiser.

Yet Talor hesitated to join his kin just yet. Before he settled down to a hot meal and a cup of ale, there was someone he wanted to see first.

Turning on his heel, Talor strode from the broch and into the village beyond. Outside, night had settled, although the fires on the walls sent out a red-hued glow over the fort. The ground inside the inner wall was slippery and slushy, but beyond a thick carpet of snow still lay upon the frozen earth. It would take a few days before it started to melt, if more snow did not fall in the meantime.

Unlike when they had arrived at Dun Ringill, the sea of conical-roofed huts and roundhouses that filled the space between the inner and outer perimeter were now occupied. Smoke rose from the slits in the sod roofs, and the aroma of cooking oatcakes filled the air.

Passing through the archway and the ruined gates, Talor turned left and made his way toward the northern edge of the village, where what remained of The Serpent tribe now resided.

An uneasy peace had settled over the fort, and Galan had taken precautions. A makeshift wooden perimeter now rose between The Serpent lodgings and the rest of the village, and a row of Eagle warriors guarded it.

They let Talor through without comment, and he made his way to the largest of the roundhouses that rose up near the northern wall.

As he approached, a tall figure ducked out of the doorway and rose to meet him.

"I had a feeling you were on your way," Mor greeted Talor. The golden light of the fires on the walls caught the red hues of her hair. As always, she wore it unbound, and the waves cascaded over the fur wrap about her shoulders.

Talor's mouth quirked. It was strong, this link between them, and he had felt it too inside the broch. He had known Mor wanted to see him, to speak to him, and so he had come to her.

Nearing Mor, Talor reached out, cupping her cheek with his hand. "How is everyone?" he asked. He noted the tension on her face, the sadness in her eyes. She had hoped to save her father, but that had not come to pass.

"Subdued ... and nervous about what the future holds," she replied. "But my uncle leads The Serpent now, and they trust him."

Talor nodded. Artair had shown courage, emerging from the broch unarmed to stand between the attackers and the last of his people.

In the aftermath of the siege, The Serpent had kept their distance from the warriors of the united tribes. Despite that Wid had backed down, animosity still ran high. It would take a while for the anger and need for revenge to settle down completely. In the meantime, everyone needed to take time to eat, drink, rest, and sleep.

Stepping closer still, Talor gazed deep into Mor's moss-green eyes. She stared back at him, unflinching, her expression softer than he had ever seen it. "Are you nervous about tomorrow?" he asked after a pause.

"No," she murmured, raising an eyebrow. "Are you?"

"Terrified."

She gave a soft laugh. "Really? This was your idea."

"Aye ... one of my better ones. Still ... I never thought I'd wed. I imagined I'd fall in battle before that day ever came."

"As did I," Mor replied, before her eyes shadowed. "You don't regret proposing to me, do you?"

Talor shook his head. "Never." He cleared his throat then, suddenly overcome. A wave of protectiveness slammed into him. "I'm not just doing this for our people, Mor. I'm too selfish for that. I'm doing this because I want *you*."

"You're not selfish," she whispered. Mor raised a hand then, cupping the fingers that cradled her cheek. "I've never met anyone more loyal, more capable of love. What you did today ... I will never forget it."

Talor smiled and stepped closer still, enfolding Mor in his arms. She came willingly, her face resting against his neck, her arms wrapping around his waist. Her nearness, the feel of her lips against the sensitive skin under his ear, inflamed Talor. His pulse quickened, and his groin started to ache. And yet he held back.

Tonight was for tenderness. Tomorrow they would be handfasted, and after that he would claim Mor as his wife.

But he could sense the blanket of sorrow that hung over Mor as he held her, and knew that she grieved for her father.

No words were needed now.

Talor tightened his hold on her, burying his face in the rosemary-scented softness of her hair. He was not going to pretend he had liked the man. If he was honest, he was pleased that the bastard was dead, and yet in the end Cathal had been prepared to sacrifice his own pride for his people. He had not deserved the death that Tormud had dealt him, stabbed in the back.

Cathal was to blame for much suffering, although he had brought his people to The Winged Isle in search of a better life. His mistake had been in thinking he could take this land from its people by brute force. His arrogance had been his undoing.

But he was Mor's father all the same, and she had loved him as much as Talor did his own father. He would not taint her memories of the man. He would hold her while she grieved for him.

And so they stood together, bodies pressed close, arms wrapped around each other, and let the healing power of the night enfold them.

Chapter Thirty

A Second Chance

TALOR AND MOR wed upon the stony beach that stretched south of Dun Ringill. A chill breeze gusted in off the water, pulling at the heavy plaid skirt that Mor had donned for the occasion. The wind ruffled Talor's short hair and tangled Mor's long tresses. With the world still carpeted in snow, there were no flowers to weave through her hair; instead, Old Murdina had presented her with sprigs of drualus—mistletoe—a sacred plant for their people. Mor wore the drualus, in a crown about her forehead, but no other adornment; they had fled with very little from their homeland.

The crone looked on now, standing at the edge of the crowd that had gathered near the waterline to watch the couple's handfasting. She wore a fey smile upon her wrinkled face, observing Ailene keenly as she unwrapped a length of plaid from around the couples joined hands. They had just made their vows to each other, and the crowd of men, women, and bairns who watched the ceremony had gone still. Mor had even heard a few sniffs, as some of the women wiped away tears.

Even though many in the fort were still wary of uniting The Eagle and The Serpent, it was a hard-hearted soul indeed who could walk away dry-eyed from a handfasting. Even Wid mac Manus had attended the ceremony, although Mor had not looked The Wolf chieftain's way since it had begun.

Despite the cold, both Talor and Mor stood barefoot on the icy stones. Mor's feet had started to ache from the chill, but she paid them no mind. Instead, her attention was wholly focused upon the dark-haired man who stood before her.

Talor mac Donnel was breathtakingly handsome this morning. Clad in black leather breeches and vest, a golden torque around his throat bearing two carven eagle heads meeting, the sight of him made Mor's breathing catch. And the fierce look on his face as he promised to stand by her side, to protect her and their children, made her chest ache.

Ailene finished removing the plaid ribbon binding them and stepped back. "You are now bound, one to the other." The seer's voice echoed out across the windy shore. Ailene then caught Talor's eye and favored him with an impish grin. "Kiss her then."

Talor grinned back at his cousin and, stepping forward, cupped Mor's face with his hands and swept in for a kiss. Mor's eyes closed, and she leaned into him, losing herself in the scent of his skin, the strength of his hands, the contained passion of his lips sliding across hers.

She was dimly aware of cheers and applause from the onlookers, but didn't pay any attention to them. Her lips parted under Talor's, and the cheering turned into a roar in her ears.

When they drew apart, the pair of them were both breathing hard.

Talor was watching her with a hot, melting stare that made Mor's knees tremble underneath her. She wanted him to drag him away, to the roundhouse in the village where they were to spend their wedding night, so that she could rip off the tight leather encasing his muscular body and feast upon him.

But their handfasting feast awaited—and it was as important for the uniting of their peoples as this ceremony had been.

For the first time The Serpent would sit down with the people of the united tribes, and would eat and drink with them. The feast symbolized the beginning of a new era for this isle and everyone upon it.

Catching Talor's hand, Mor turned, her gaze taking in the crowd that formed a semi-circle around them on the shore. They were all there: Artair and a handful of her own people, as well as all four of the chieftains of the united tribes and their kin.

Talor's cousin, Fina, stood near the front of the crowd, her husband's arm around her shoulders. Fina's eyes gleamed as she watched them, and for a moment the two women's gazes fused.

Warmth filtered through Mor. She had liked Fina from their first meeting, as she had Ailene. The past year had been a lonely time for Mor; after losing her mother, she'd had few other female companions. Instead, she had spent all her time with her father, uncle, and brothers. She missed the company of other women, and as Fina's mouth curved into a smile, Mor knew that the pair of them would become close friends.

Smoke hung in the air inside the broch, the pungent smell of burning peat mingling with the savory aromas of roasted venison, braised onions, and freshly baked bread. The strains of a harp floated through the space, barely audible at times as the rumble of conversation rose and fell throughout the hall.

Seated next to Talor, Mor took it all in. As the newly wedded couple, they sat upon the raised platform at one end of the hall, a position usually reserved for The Eagle chieftain and his kin. This afternoon though, all the chieftains—including her uncle—sat at the table with them, while everyone else sat upon low benches at long tables that lined the hall, forming a great square around the huge hearth.

"Quite a sight, isn't it?" Talor whispered in her ear. The tickle of his breath against her skin made Mor's breathing quicken. She turned to her husband, her mouth curving. "Aye ... one that warms my heart." She paused then, lowering her gaze as the events of the past days revisited her. "There were times when I despaired, when I thought it might never happen."

"But you never gave up," he replied. "You fought right till the end."

Talor reached forward then and picked up a jug of bramble wine, pouring them both some. "Are you ready to drink from our wedding cups?"

Mor raised her chin, smiling. She had forgotten about this tradition; it had been a while since she had been a guest at a handfasting. There had been no time for such things among her people for a while—not with their very survival at stake. "Aye, go on then."

Together, they picked up their cups, interlaced their arms, and raised the rims to their own lips. Mor took a sip, sighing as the rich, spicy wine slid down her throat. Meanwhile, Talor's gaze held hers, his eyes full of sensual promise. She felt the tension in his body, in the thigh that pressed up against hers; he was as eager as her for their wedding night.

Lowering their cups, they began to eat from the platter they shared. The venison was delicious, flavored with flakes of salt and rosemary. Mor ate slowly, savoring each mouthful, yet all the while her awareness of the man next to her grew, and the excitement that flickered in the pit of her belly reminded her that the true hunger within her was not for food and drink, but for the man seated next to her.

Mor fed Talor a piece of venison, her core starting to ache as he licked the meat juices off her fingers.

Getting through this feast without bursting into flames was going to be torture.

A few feet away, Galan mac Muin rose to his feet. At the sight of The Eagle chieftain looming above them, a drinking horn in his hand, the rumble of conversation and music faded into silence.

Galan waited till he had everyone's attention, before he cleared his throat and held his drinking horn high. "Today marks a turning point in our history," he said, his gruff voice echoing high into the rafters. "It shows us all that some good can come from tragedy, and that you can always start again, even when all hope seems lost."

Galan paused there, and Mor saw that the chieftain's cheeks were slightly flushed. That was his second horn of mead, and although he usually appeared a quiet, self-contained man, the drink had loosened his tongue.

"I grew up in the shadow of war," Galan continued, his iron-grey gaze sweeping around the hall. "And my father fell in a battle against The Wolf. We were once bitter enemies ... the fighting had gone on for so long that none of us could even remember what had started the blood feud between us. But when my father fell, I swore to myself that I would break the cycle." Galan cast a warm glance at the dark-haired woman who was seated beside him. "I wed Tea, and together we helped bring our peoples together."

A few feet farther down the table, Mor saw Wid mac Manus shift in his seat. Although The Wolf chieftain no longer looked like he wanted to throw himself at Mor and strangle her with his bare hands, the warrior wore a shuttered expression this afternoon. He tolerated this union, but she sensed that deep down he was not happy about it. Next to him, Wid's wife cast her husband a soft smile, placing a hand over his upon the table before him.

However, Galan had not yet finished his speech. He turned his attention now to where Varar and Fina sat at the far end of the table. "But as much as I wanted peace with my neighbors, I could not bring it about ... no sooner had relations improved with The Wolf when we clashed with The Boar."

Farther down the table, Galan's brother Tarl gave a small smile. He sat next to an exotically beautiful woman with jet-black hair and golden skin. This must have been Lucrezia, Fina's mother—a woman of the Caesars. Mor watched him with interest, before her attention shifted to Talor's father, Donnel, who sat a few feet away. Talor had told her of what had taken place twenty years earlier—of the rift between the two tribes that had nearly brought them to open war. Varar's uncles had made enemies of Tarl and Donnel, and the tribes had come close to another bitter feud.

"I thought history would repeat itself with you, Varar," Galan said, addressing The Boar chieftain directly now. "But, like your father, you could see beyond the grievances that have steeped our isle in blood for so many years."

Galan broke off then, a rare smile stretching his face. He was a striking man when serious, but incredibly handsome when he smiled, Mor noted. All three of the mac Muin brothers were pleasing on the eye—it was no wonder that Talor was so attractive. "I am rambling," he admitted. "The mead has loosened my tongue, I'm afraid ... but my sentiments are real. For a while now, I have grown increasingly bitter, sure that my dream of peace would never come to pass." A beat passed as Galan's gaze then rested upon Mor. "But thanks to you, Mor, it has. Raise your cups everyone ... to peace."

"To peace!" The shouts echoed high into the rafters. Mor took a sip of wine, swallowing the lump that had just formed in her throat; she had no idea that The Eagle chieftain felt that way.

"The four chieftains of the united tribes have discussed what happens now," Galan continued when silence settled once more, his attention never leaving Mor. "And The Eagle and The Boar have decided that we will make a gift of Kyleakin and the surrounding lands to what remains of your people. Artair mac Calum will lead

The Serpent there, and ... of course ... you and Talor are
welcome to join him."

A wide smile stretched across Mor's face. She tore her
gaze from Galan's and met her uncle's farther down the
table. He too was smiling, although there was no
surprise in his eyes.

The chieftains had already discussed their decision
with him.

Setting down her cup, Mor rose to her feet. All around
the feasting hall, faces swiveled to her, and Mor let her
own gaze travel over them all, picking out every face that
lined the long tables beneath the platform. She then
shifted her attention to the faces of the four men who
had made the decision to gift her people Kyleakin.
"Thank you," she said huskily. "This is more than I dared
hope for ... thank you for giving my people a second
chance."

Chapter Thirty-one

That's How Fate Works

TALOR'S GAZE FEASTED upon Mor as she lowered herself back down onto her seat. A flush had spread across her high cheekbones, and her eyes gleamed with emotion. Her crown of drualus still sat upon her head, the small white berries and dark green leaves contrasting with the russet of her hair.

She had never looked so beautiful.

The ache in his groin intensified. Although he appreciated his uncle's impassioned speech, this was turning into the longest feast he had ever attended. Handfasting celebrations were known to be lengthy affairs, often lasting late into the night.

It would be a while yet, before he and Mor would be allowed to leave the hall and retire to their roundhouse in the village. His uncle had offered them an alcove in the broch, yet Talor had asked to be given a roundhouse instead. He had grown up in one with his father and Eithni, and found the alcoves where most of his kin resided stifling.

He wanted Mor and him to have their own space while they resided here in Dun Ringill.

Talor drew in a deep breath and tried to focus on the food that he had no appetite for.

Patience. It was not something he had ever excelled at.

The feasting drew out, and more mead, wine, and ale flowed. Then oatcakes dripping with butter and honey were served. In handfasting tradition, the newlyweds fed each other pieces of cake.

Doing so, nearly unraveled what remained of Talor's self-restraint, especially when Mor licked honey off his fingers. The sight of her pink tongue sliding across the base of his thumb caused Talor to choke back a moan. His shaft now strained against the tight leather breeches he wore. He would not be able to stand up right now without embarrassing himself.

Around them men and women rose to their feet and started to push back the tables and benches, readying the floor for dancing.

Frustration pulsed through Talor at the sight. He did not want to dance. He wanted to plow his wife, and he had nearly reached the limits of his endurance.

At the end of the raised platform, he spied his step-mother, Eithni, taking a seat at her beloved harp, while his aunt, Tea, pulled up a stool beside her. A moment later Eithni's fingers started to fly across the strings, and Tea's beautiful voice soared. They sang a ballad he knew well—one about a lass of the fair folk who fell in love with a mortal man and the tragic tale that followed. Despite that it was a song of love and loss, it was haunting in its beauty.

As the song reached its conclusion, Talor stole a glance at his wife. Mor was watching Eithni and Tea, her attention rapt, as tears trickled down her face.

"Have you never heard that song before?" Talor asked softly. Leaning close, he wiped away her tears with a gentle sweep of his knuckles.

Mor shook her head. "We haven't had a lot of time of late for music and songs … and no one among my people can sing like that."

Talor smiled. "My aunt has a voice to make the Gods weep."

The song concluded then, and Eithni and Tea struck up another—this one a jaunty tune about a lecherous farmer and his many lovers. Couples flowed out onto the dance floor, laughter echoing out into the hall.

Talor grasped Mor's hand then and rose to his feet, pulling Mor with him.

Her eyes flew open wide. "You want to dance?"

"No," he said, the need to be away from this hall, and alone with her, turning him terse. "I want *you*."

Mor's eyes widened further still, before a wicked smile curved her mouth. "Isn't it too early to leave?"

"Aye … but we're leaving all the same."

Those at the chieftain's table cheered as the couple stepped down from the platform. They assumed that Talor was leading his wife onto the floor to join the dancers. But, gripping Mor's hand tightly, Talor took her straight past them, hauled open the door, and led her out into the night. Hooting and catcalls followed them, as the revelers realized what Talor intended.

Ignoring the cheering, Talor pulled the door shut after them and, hand in hand, they descended the stone steps into the yard beyond.

After the hot, smoky air within the hall, the cold air outdoors hit Talor like a slap across the face. He inhaled a deep lungful of it all the same, enjoying its freshness. The stillness of the night was a balm after the noise inside the broch.

Neither of them spoke as they crossed the yard and passed under the archway into the village. No sound but the crunch of their boots on the snow followed them. Most of the occupants of Dun Ringill were packed into the broch, and those who were not were slumbering in their furs.

The roundhouse sat a few yards away from the south gate. As he approached, Talor remembered the last time he had walked this way—it had been when Mor had freed him during that blizzard.

Only a few days had passed since their escape, and yet it felt like a lifetime ago. Talor felt like a different man. His entire way of looking at life had shifted, and it was all because of the woman who clung to his hand.

They entered the roundhouse, stepping out of the cold into a warm space that smelled of dried heather and rosemary. A hearth glowed in the center of the circular room, and glancing down, Talor saw that someone had strewn herbs over the floor, hence the scent that had greeted them.

A few feet away, a huge pile of soft furs awaited.

Talor turned to Mor, aware that his heart was hammering so violently against his chest that it felt as if it might burst free. He had never had this reaction before bedding a woman. Desire galloped through him, and as their gazes fused, he felt his shaft swell once more, turning rock-hard and painful in the constraints of his breeches.

Mor only had to fix him with that sultry look of hers, and his body reacted, violently.

Murmuring a curse, Talor pulled her into his arms and gave her the kiss he had been dying to bestow upon her since their handfasting ceremony. His hands roamed Mor's strong, lush body—down the long curve of her back to the globes of her buttocks—as his tongue plunged into her mouth and tangled with hers.

Mor tasted like heather honey, her mouth as hungry as his. Her hands pulled at his clothing, her fingers fumbling when she unlaced his vest and pushed it off him. Likewise, he unlaced the plaid bodice she wore. The garment flattered Mor beautifully, for it pushed up her full breasts, revealing a deep cleavage and an expanse of creamy skin that had been enticing him all day. But he preferred her naked.

The firelight played across her full breasts and rose-pink nipples. They strained up toward him, the nipples pebbling hard under his hot gaze.

With a groan, Talor caught her breasts in his hands, pushing them up to meet his mouth. This was what he had wanted to feast on; there was nothing more delicious.

Mor let out a soft whimper—a sound that excited him beyond measure—her fingers running through his hair. Her fingertips then dug into his scalp, urging him on.

He suckled her hard, until she gave another cry, her body trembling against him. Pulling back from her, Talor struggled to keep a rein on his self-control. He prided himself on his ability to draw a love-making session out, but right now he just wanted to throw Mor back on the furs, part her thighs, and plow her until she screamed for mercy.

She unraveled him completely.

Sensing his conflict, a sultry smile stretched Mor's lips. And then she dropped to her knees before him and reached up to unlace his breeches.

His shaft sprang free to meet her, eager to be loosed of its tight leather prison, and Mor was on it in an instant, her mouth greedily taking him in, right to the hilt.

"Gods," Talor choked out, his hands tangling in her hair. "Go slow ... I can't ... Mor!"

The heat of her mouth, the sensual ministrations of her lips and tongue, were too much. Talor exploded, his body arching as he spilled into her mouth. His cry shuddered through the dwelling.

Breathing hard, he pulled Mor to her feet. She licked her lips before smiling, pleased that she had caused him to lose control like that. Talor was used to being in charge in the furs—no woman had ever taken him in hand so confidently, had ever taken him over the brink so swiftly.

And yet his rod was still rock-hard.

He was done waiting.

Reaching down, he undid the belt at Mor's waist and stripped it off, before pushing down the heavy plaid skirt so that it pooled on the floor. The sight of her long, strong, naked body made lust surge through his loins once more. He had to be inside her. Right now.

"Get on the furs," he growled, "and spread your legs for me."

Mor's breasts heaved as her breathing caught. She watched his eyes darken, her lips parting with arousal. She loved it when he was dominant in the furs; he had seen it during their first coupling. Mor was strong and independent, a warrior to be reckoned with, yet she liked to give up control when she was with him.

She wanted him to take her hard. Once again, Talor usually preferred slow, languorous lovemaking. But with Mor it was different—somehow this woman unleashed the beast within him.

Mor moved back, never taking her gaze from his, and lowered herself onto the furs. Then slowly, deliberately, she spread her creamy thighs, revealing herself to him.

For an instant Talor merely stared, his groin aching now—ready for her again—and then he lunged for her.

Grabbing her knees, he pushed her legs back hard and sheathed himself inside her with one deep thrust.

Mor's answering cry drove him wild. He plunged into her, his fingers biting into her soft thighs as he slid into her heat again and again. Within moments he was lost. He rode her savagely, but Mor answered him thrust for thrust. Her groans and cries, as she writhed against him, were Talor's undoing. This woman was so lusty, so wild. She set fire to his blood in a way he had never experienced before.

And when she shuddered under him, her body arching, the feel of her heat tightening around him sent Talor over the edge. His hoarse cries mingled with hers.

"Talor mac Donnel," Mor murmured, tracing her fingertips down Talor's sweat-slicked back, "that was ... like being caught up in a tempest."

"Gods, woman," he rasped, his face buried in her neck. "You will stop my heart if every time is like that."

Mor chuckled. "A warrior's death indeed."

Still breathing hard, Talor pushed himself up off her, propping himself up on an elbow. In the light of the firepit just a few feet away, his face was achingly handsome, his gaze fathomless.

"There is no way I'd rather go," he murmured, his mouth quirking in that way that made her loins melt. He was still buried inside her, and already she could feel him beginning to harden once more. Her core responded with a pulsing ache that made her stifle a groan.

Talor reached out then and traced her cheek with his fingers. To Mor's surprise, she saw his hand trembled slightly. She had been rocked by their stormy lovemaking, but she now realized that he had been similarly affected.

"I love you, Mor," he said, his voice roughening with emotion. "I know it might seem sudden, for me to tell you this, but it's the truth."

Mor stared up at him, her own breathing quickening. "And I love you," she whispered, reaching up and tracing his full lower lip with a fingertip. It was true, the tenderness within her chest felt as if it might burst. "What you said yesterday was right. Our fates have been entwined since we both came into this world. Neither of us should be surprised that it has come to this."

Talor's eyes gleamed, and his throat bobbed. "What did I do to deserve you?"

Mor smiled. "Nothing, mo ghràdh. That's how fate works. I was born to be yours, Talor mac Donnel, and you to be mine."

Epilogue

A Fine Place to Call Home

Mid-summer, 390 AD
Kyleakin—territory of The Serpent

6 months later ...

"MUIN AND AILENE are here!" Mor burst into the hall, face flushed with excitement. "I've just seen them approach from the west."

Talor glanced up from the scattering of bones upon the table and raised an eyebrow. "Are you sure it's them? They're not due till tomorrow."

"I have the eyesight of a hawk," Mor replied, placing her hands upon her hips and fixing him with a level look he had come to know well. "If you don't believe me, come and check for yourself."

Varar chuckled at that, pushing himself up from the long table where the two men had been sharing cups of mead and trying to best each other at knucklebones. "Great ... an excuse to end this torture."

Talor huffed. "Don't you enjoy knucklebones?"

"I enjoy *winning* at knucklebones ... that's not the same thing."

"Come on." Mor turned on her heel and strode from the hall. "Let's go out to meet them."

Talor rose to his feet and, with a grin at Varar, followed his wife outside. The Boar chieftain, who had arrived with Fina the day before, fell into step with him. They left the large round-tower that dominated the northern edge of the village and stepped outdoors, to be greeted with a golden afternoon. Sunlight sparkled off the water of the great channel that separated The Winged Isle from the mainland beyond, and the mountains to the west were tawny in the afternoon sun.

Mid-Summer Fire, which celebrated the shortest night and the longest day of the year, was just a day away now.

Their first in Kyleakin.

They had built a great bonfire in the meadow south of the settlement: a mound of branches and twigs, which they would set alight tomorrow after dusk. Then the folk of Kyleakin would drink ale, eat cakes studded with berries and nuts, and dance around the pyre.

Talor smiled in anticipation. He and Mor had traveled here for the first fire festival of the year, Earth Fire, and had remained to help Artair make this place a proper home for their people.

Our people.

Warmth seeped through Talor's chest as these words settled over him. A handful of Eagle and Boar folk had joined them here, but most of those living at Kyleakin were survivors from the siege of Dun Ringill. At first, he had kept apart from many of the people here, allowing Mor to have dealings with them. But as the moons had passed, and the last of the bitter weather departed, Talor had worked shoulder to shoulder with Serpent warriors as they repaired the wooden palisade that ringed Kyleakin.

And he had discovered he had more in common with them than he realized.

"It's a good spot this," Varar commented as they walked through the scattering of low-slung huts. "The land is fertile, and you are close to the mountains for hunting."

"You're *always* close to the mountains on this isle," Talor reminded him with a smile. That was why the weather was so changeable here; the union of the mountains and the sea brought with it wild storms, heavy snows, and long foggy days where the sun never showed its face.

"You don't miss Dun Ringill?"

Talor shook his head. "I thought I would ... but as soon as I got settled here, I haven't. The only thing I miss is my kin."

As Talor spoke these last words, he spied two figures ride in upon shaggy ponies through the gates. He recognized them both instantly: Muin and Ailene.

Mor and Fina had already reached the newcomers.

Ailene swung down from her pony and rushed over to Fina, throwing her arms around her. It was difficult to give Fina a proper hug these days though, for her belly was starting to swell considerably. She was due at Gateway, as bairns often were—a high number of children were conceived during the bitter season, for during those months folk remained indoors for long periods, with little else to do but spend time together in the furs.

Mor hung back while Fina and Ailene embraced, although it warmed Talor to see that his cousin threw her arms around his wife next. Before they had departed from Dun Ringill, Mor had become good friends with his cousins, the three of them often inseparable. There had been tears when they parted ways. Fina had returned to An Teanga with Varar, Ailene had remained at Dun Ringill with Muin, while Mor and Talor had departed for Kyleakin.

They had all set off upon different paths in life now—and yet it made their reunions all the sweeter.

Muin leaped down from his pony, covering the ground in long strides, as he approached Talor. Meeting his cousin halfway, Talor embraced him, although Muin's grip nearly cracked his ribs. Varar stepped forward then, and the pair clasped arms—a traditional greeting between male warriors among their people—as they grinned at each other.

"You're early," Talor noted, rubbing his ribs. Muin did not know his own strength at times.

Muin huffed. "Ailene insisted we leave in advance … she's been going on about this trip for the last moon. In the end, I gave in."

Talor laughed, his gaze shifting back to where the three women now approached. Mor, dressed in tight-fitting leather breeches and a plaid tunic belted at the waist, led the way. It had been a hot day, and so his wife had braided her hair and coiled it high upon her head, revealing a long, slender neck.

Even after six moons together, the sight of her made Talor's pulse quicken. The passing of time had only added to the passion he felt for this woman, and had deepened the bond forged between them.

Talor discovered that Mor was easy to live with—she had an independent spirit and as such did not seek to control those around her. She let Talor be, giving him the space he liked, and as a result, he was constantly looking for excuses to spend time with her.

"I told you it was them," Mor said, stepping up to Talor's side.

Reaching out, he pulled her to him, placing a protective arm around her waist. "Aye, you did," he replied.

Ailene reached them then, flinging her arms around Talor's neck and slapping a kiss on his cheek. Drawing back, she ran an assessing eye over him. "You're looking well, cousin." Her mouth quirked then. "I thought you might have pined for us a bit."

Next to her, Muin snorted. "I think not … he couldn't wait to leave Dun Ringill for pastures new."

Ailene swung her gaze around, taking in the small dirt square inside the gates where they stood. Fowl pecked and scratched at the dusty ground, and a few yards away, a woman gathered in washing from a line, singing as she worked. "It's nice here."

"It's home," Mor replied, her arm snaking around Talor's waist. "There was quite a bit of damage to be repaired, but the last of it has been done now."

Silence followed these words, and Mor's gaze shadowed. Talor knew what she was thinking.

The Serpent horde had initially landed near Kyleakin, and as such the settlement had borne the brunt of their first attack. The village had been abandoned then, as what remained of its inhabitants fled. It was an irony—but somehow fitting—that it was The Serpent who had rebuilt its walls once more.

"Aye, and Kyleakin now prospers again," Fina said, breaking the silence. Her gaze was warm as it settled upon Mor. "I'm glad it feels like home to you now."

"I'm parched," Muin spoke up. "I hope your ale is as good as ours."

Talor snorted. "It's better." He gestured toward where the stack-stoned round-tower they had repaired since their arrival loomed over the village. "Come on ... let's open a fresh barrel."

The party moved toward the round-tower. Varar and Fina led the way, arm in arm, while Muin and Ailene followed closed behind. Their voices drifted back through the collection of huts, where children played outside. Most of the folk of Kyleakin were still out in the fields, but they would return shortly as the shadows lengthened, and the village would be bustling once more.

Talor and Mor trailed behind their visitors, enjoying a rare moment alone. Up ahead, Talor spied Artair appear in the doorway of the round-tower, leaning on his crutch as always. He had been taking an afternoon nap when Muin and Ailene arrived. He waved to them now, a smile stretching across his face.

"Your uncle seems a lot happier these days," Talor noted. "When he first arrived here, I rarely saw him smile."

"He was heart-sore after losing my father," Mor replied, her voice turning introspective. "But like me, he knows he has a lot to be grateful for. Kyleakin is a fine place to call home."

"Do you ever long for the mainland?" Talor asked, deliberately slowing his step so that the others drew farther ahead. Since Varar and Fina's arrival, they had barely had time to chat together as they usually did.

Mor shook her head. "I miss my kin ... my parents and brothers ... but little else."

"One day we shall have a family of our own, Mor," Talor reminded her gently. In the past moons he had hoped her womb would quicken; they had certainly coupled often enough to warrant it. "Hopefully that will ease your heart."

Mor drew to a halt then, turning to him. She met Talor's eye, her mouth curving into a sly smile. "That day will arrive perhaps sooner than you think." When Talor stared back at her uncomprehending, she gave a frustrated huff. "My moonflow never came. I visited the healer this morning, and she assures me I am with bairn."

Joy exploded through Talor, with a force that caused him to inhale sharply. "Is she certain of this?"

Mor's smile widened. "As certain as she can be." She moved closer then, leaning in. Her lips brushed his cheek, her breath feathering against the shell of his ear as she whispered to him. "Will I give you a daughter or a son?"

Talor wrapped his arms around Mor, yanking her hard against him. She squealed, causing the others up ahead to stop and look back. However, Talor ignored them. Instead, his mouth slanted over Mor's, and he kissed her deeply.

When he finally broke away, he saw that his wife's green eyes were shining. She was as delighted as he was about the news.

"Either will do me fine," Talor said, before he captured her mouth with his once more.

"Come on ... you can kiss your wife later," Muin called from where he had stopped before the doors to the round-tower. "How about that ale? I'm dying of thirst here."

With a sigh, Talor drew back from Mor. Then, looping an arm around her shoulders, he steered her toward the others. "Very well," he called out to his cousin. "Although, we have something besides your arrival to celebrate. Come inside ... Mor and I have news to share."

The End.

From the author

And here we arrive at the end of THE PICT WARS series—and the end of a journey that began with BLOOD FEUD and THE WARRIOR BROTHERS OF SKYE series.

The two trilogies can be read as a six-book series—and I hope you loved the stories as much as I did. I'm in love with The Winged Isle and the brave men and women who inhabited this wild land. The Pict history and culture holds a great fascination for me, and I adored bringing it to life with these books.

Although I've written enemies to lovers stories before, this one felt a bit different. It's also a story about revenge, a quest for peace, and an exploration of the different ways we handle grief. In addition I explore the idea that someone can truly be 'meant' for you.

It takes a lot of strength and courage required to stand up for your beliefs, even when the whole world is against you. For this reason, Mor is probably one of my favorite heroines yet. She's a warrior, but there's a calm strength and determination in her that I admired. This novel's happy ending is largely her doing. Talor was her perfect partner—and it was great fun bringing them together.

I'll be taking a break from the Picts now, as I focus on a new series set in Medieval Scotland. But I'll be staying on the Isle of Skye though ... I've loved using this island as the setting of my novels. The dramatic landscape and rich history make it the perfect backdrop for romance!

I'm also going to be merging a little bit of Dark Ages and Medieval Scotland in a Historical Fantasy Romance series scheduled for later in 2020. Want a few clues about the new series? Three Roman centurions. A witch's curse. Immortality. And Medieval Scotland. Are you as excited as I am about this? Make sure you join my mailing list or follow me on Facebook to keep updated (links below).

If you're new to my books, make sure you check out THE BRIDES OF SKYE series (also set in Medieval Isle of Skye) and my new series THE SISTERS OF KILBRIDE.

Thank you so much for reading my books, and I hope you love them as much as I do!

Jayne x

Historical and background notes for WARRIOR'S WRATH

Glossary

Aos Sí or Fair Folk: fairies
bandruí: a female druid or seer
Broch: a tall, round, stone-built, hollow-walled Iron Age tower-house
Caesars: the Ancient Romans
mo ghràdh: my love
mo leannan: my lover, my sweetheart.

Place names

An t-Eilean Sgitheanach: Gaelic name for the Isle of Skye
Dun Ardtreck: a broch located on the Minginish Peninsula of Skye
Dun Ringill: an Iron Age hill fort on the Strathaird Peninsula of Skye
An Teanga: an Iron Age broch located on the southern coast of Skye
Dun Grianan: an Iron Age broch located on the north-western coast of Skye
Balintur: village in the north of The Eagle territory
The Black Cuillins: mountain range in the Isle of Skye
The Valley of the Tors: a valley that marks the border of The Eagle and The Boar territories
Kyleakin: a settlement on the south-eastern coast of the Isle of Skye

The four tribes of The Winged Isle*

The People of The Eagle (south-west)
The People of The Wolf (north-west)

The People of The Boar (south-east)
The People of The Stag (north-east)

Gods and Goddesses of The Winged Isle*

The Mother: Goddess of enlightenment and feminine
energy—the bringer of change
The Warrior: God of battle, life and growth, of summer
The Maiden: Young goddess of nature and fertility
The Hag: Goddess of the dark—sleep, dreams, death,
winter, and the earth
The Reaper: God of death

Festivities on the Isle of Skye*

Earth Fire: Salute to new life and the first signs of spring
(February 1)
Bealtunn: Spring Equinox
Mid-Summer Fire: Summer Equinox
Harvest Fire: Festival to salute the harvest (Aug 1)
Gateway: Passage from summer to winter (October
31/November 1)
Mid-Winter Fire: Winter Equinox

* Author's note: I have taken 'artistic license' when it
comes to the names of the tribes, festivities, and gods
and goddesses upon the Isle of Skye. The historical
evidence is very scant, making it a challenge for me to
get an accurate picture of what the names of the tribes
living upon Skye during the 4th century would have
been. Likewise I could not find any references to their
gods and festivities. The Picts were an enigmatic people,
and we only have their ruins and symbols to cast light on
how they lived and whom they worshipped. To make my
setting as authentic as possible, I have studied the rituals
and religions of the Celtic peoples of Scotland, Ireland,
and Wales of a similar period and have created a culture
I feel could have existed.

The culture, language, and religion of the Picts is one largely shrouded in mystery. Unlike my novels set in 7th Century Anglo-Saxon England, which is a reasonably well-documented period, researching 4th Century Isle of Skye proved to be a challenge. Pictish culture is largely an enigma to us. However, they did leave behind a number of fascinating stone ruins, standing stones, and artifacts, as well as a detailed collection of symbolic art.

I created the four tribes of The Winged Isle from Pictish animal symbols. This is not a far-fetched idea; many Iron and Bronze-age peoples identified themselves with animal symbols. The clans we identify with Scotland did not appear until a few centuries later.

Cast of characters
For those of you who have read THE WARRIOR BROTHERS OF SKYE, understanding who is who in THE PICT WARS shouldn't be too much of a stretch. However, I am aware that my cast of characters is gradually expanding (especially since I've now thrown another tribe into the mix!). So here are all the characters, and their relationships to each other, categorized by tribe:

The Eagle tribe
Galan mac Muin: Eagle chieftain wed to **Tea** with two sons, **Muin** and **Aaron**.
Tarl mac Muin: younger brother of The Eagle chieftain, wed to **Lucrezia** with one daughter, **Fina** (they had three sons who died in childhood: **Bradhg, Fionn**, and **Ciaran**)
Donnel mac Muin: youngest brother of The Eagle chieftain, wed to **Eithni** (healer) with one son and two daughters: **Talor** (son from his first marriage), **Bonnie** (deceased), and **Eara**
Ailene: the seer at Dun Ringill

The Boar tribe
Varar mac Urcal: Boar chieftain wed to Fina.

Urcal mac Wrad: previous Boar chieftain – the eldest
of three sons: **Wurgest** and **Loxa** (all three deceased)
Morag: Varar's sister

The Wolf tribe
Wid mac Manus: Wolf chieftain, wed to **Alana** with
two sons, **Calum** and **Bred** (deceased).
Fingal mac Diarmid: Wolf warrior

The Stag tribe
Tadhg mac Fortrenn: Stag chieftain, wed to **Erea**
with two daughters, **Moira** and **Ana**

The Cruthini (The Serpent tribe)
Cathal mac Calum: Serpent chieftain
Artair: Cathal's brother
Mor: Cathal's daughter
Murdina: seer
Dunchadh (deceased) and **Tamhas** (deceased):
Cathal's sons
Tormud mac Alec: Boar warrior, now a member of
The Serpent tribe

About the Author

Ja Award-winning author Jayne Castel writes epic Historical and Fantasy Romance. Her vibrant characters, richly researched historical settings and action-packed adventure romance transport readers to forgotten times and imaginary worlds.

Jayne is the author of the Amazon bestselling BRIDES OF SKYE series—a Medieval Scottish Romance trilogy about three strong-willed sisters and the men who love them. An exciting spin-off series set in the same story-world, THE SISTERS OF KILBRIDE, is now available as well. In love with all things Scottish, Jayne also writes romances set in Dark Ages Scotland ... sexy Pict warriors anyone?

When she's not writing, Jayne is reading (and re-reading) her favorite authors, cooking Italian feasts, and taking her dog, Juno, for walks. She lives in New Zealand's beautiful South Island.

Connect with Jayne online:
www.jaynecastel.com
Email: contact@jaynecastel.com

www.ingramcontent.com/pod-product-compliance
Lightning Source LLC
Chambersburg PA
CBHW032250070726
47590CB00016B/1978